SASHA HIBBS

Evernight Teen ®

www.evernightteen.com

Copyright© 2025

Sasha Hibbs

ISBN: 978-0-3695-1258-1

Cover Artist: Jay Aheer

Editor: Melissa Hosack

SASHA HIBBS

DEDICATION

For my parents, Maurice and Linda Helfin, who never truly left us. And for my daughters, Aeliza and Ava Hibbs. My parents live on through them. For Zelda, the unearthly creature the universe sent our family to guide us through some of the darkest times. Hers is a light that will never go out.

ACKNOWLEDGEMENTS

I want to thank my publisher, Evernight Teen, for the creative freedom they allow and for the support they give to me as an author. I appreciate the entire team, and it takes a village. I appreciate all the editors, the cover artist (Jay Aheer who is second to none), and fellow writers that make up the team.

Of course, a giant *thank you* to my family. I wrote this during 2023-2024, at a time when I fought to stay alive. There were times I wasn't sure I'd leave the hospital, and I was afraid. I was scared my children wouldn't know how much I loved them, or my husband, and that I'd live this exact life over and over again if I only could. I'm so grateful I came out the other end of 2024 alive, thankful, appreciating all the things that I once thought were little that are so enormous to me now.

Thank you to those who inspired these pages—Valerie Jordan, an angel of a lady who truly is the human embodiment of pure joy. My girls, my nieces, their friends … all sources of creative inspiration. Thank you to my darling, darling husband, Tim. You are my sunbeams, starbursts, and magic dust.

THE TRUTH ABOUT FIREFLIES

Sasha Hibbs

Copyright © 2025

Chapter One

When A Siren Calls

Brayden

It's odd how you go your entire life oblivious, in some kind of peaceful, unknowing state. Content. Until the thing you hadn't realized was missing is now gone. It creates a void. A gnawing, aching void. Trying to fill it up is like chasing your tail, this never-ending cycle I couldn't seem to break.

I'd known Laurel Bennett since freshman year, but only from a passing distance. I knew her enough to recognize her in Walmart, or at the park, pick her out of a lineup. Like I could identify her if I had to. But I didn't know-know her until last summer. And she crashed into me faster and harder than any defensive linebacker I'd encountered in six years of playing football.

She knew where to hit me.

But the first hit, that very first time… I closed my eyes and behind my eyelids burst that memory that has tortured me day in and day out.

My parents were out of town for the weekend visiting relatives in Ohio, and with my older brother in college but hanging out with friends since he was in for the summer, it was only me. I was hungry and left to fend for myself. I'd decided on tacos. Who doesn't love tacos?

It was what my mom always called the golden hour, that hour before the sun sets, and the entire sky is streaked in bursts of yellow and fuchsia. I drove through Burrito Buns and absentmindedly watched the golden hour while scarfing down tacos.

Afterward, I wanted a hot fudge sundae. I needed to walk off some of the greasy food I'd ingested, so I decided to park my truck and walk down Main Street to the Dairy Duchess only to eat more bad decisions.

My head was in football mode, thinking about all the carbs I'd just downed, and already regretting the additional calories I was getting ready to consume, when I heard something that was haunting and captivating all at the same time. A melody that somehow grounded me right in front of this pizza joint I probably should've eaten at instead.

I couldn't move.

A slow tune was being lifted up, up, up. A guitar? No. I tilted my head. A ukulele, I believed. But something happened, some strange sensation unfurled in me when I heard the voice that went along with the tune. As though a siren sat somewhere calling to me, feet that moments ago had been cemented to the sidewalk now seemed to move of their own accord. I found myself leaning up against the Chase Bank wall, held completely captive by a girl.

There were other people around watching and listening to her. She sat perched on this flower planter with her legs dangling, red converse sneakers resting on top an open case lid where people were tipping her.

The sun was truly beginning to set, and there was the combination of dying sunlight hitting her hair just right, along with her eerie voice, which was completely hypnotizing. My chest was warm, my body relaxed.

I knew her. Knew of her was more like it. We didn't have any classes together, but I vaguely remembered her.

Laurel Bennett.

She was the homeschooled kid.

I remember when she started with our class in freshman year. Of course, there were all kinds of stories that circulated just like with anyone who was new. Rumors upon rumors. Her mom died so she came to live with her dad was one story. Another was that child protective services got involved and forced her dad into her going to school. And then we all heard at some point that Laurel simply wanted to come to school. Rumor had it she was emo, then it was that she was a stuck-up snot.

These were all things said about her.

I didn't know the truth or lies in any of them.

I'd never given her any real consideration until this very moment. And I couldn't take my eyes off her.

Her long blonde hair fell over one shoulder, and her bright eyes, her animated face, the movement of her lips as she sang—they all held me in this weird frozen relaxed place. I didn't know Laurel Bennett, but I knew I never wanted her to stop playing that little guitar and singing about broken hearts.

Unfortunately, she did stop singing. Her song was over, but the spell lingered. People dispersed, but I just couldn't bring myself to leave.

"Thank you, thank you," she said in a soft voice as people threw quarters, loose change, and a few dollar bills inside her open case.

Soon it was just me. I was her audience. As the last bit of daylight fled, she flicked her gaze to me while tuning her ukulele.

"Anything you'd like to hear?" she asked, lowering her gaze back down to the neck of her instrument while turning the knobs at the top.

I froze, mouth gaping, not sure what to say.

She looked back up at me and smiled.

Laurel was … beautiful.

My heart started hammering. My palms were sweaty. Why couldn't I think? If I were in the middle of a game, I would've already been sacked.

Think. Think. Think.

"Oh, uh, I was getting ice cream." Sweet Jesus, I couldn't have sounded any more stupid.

"Well, you're in luck," she said, still smiling. "There's a Dairy Duchess just down there." She looked down Main Street and I could see the big neon sign. She had to know I knew there was a Dairy Duchess. If you lived in Buckhannon, nothing was a surprise. You were aware of every place in Buckhannon's city limits.

"Yeah," I said, ready to panic. Instead, I hurried over to her case, threw in the five-dollar bill that was going to get my sundae and I got the hell outta there.

I could feel her eyes burning holes in my back. Not in a bad way, just in a confused sort of way. I mean, I had no idea what the hell possessed me, but I couldn't have sounded any more like a stuttering idiot.

I had all the confidence in the world on the football field. I understood strategy. I had a keen sense of defense, of playing with others, of when and what to tackle.

But I was way out of my element here.

As I hopped back up into my truck, I sat for several minutes just digesting the strange experience I had. That tune, her voice … the way she confidently yet shyly engaged in a conversation with me. Suddenly, Laurel Bennett was all I could think of.

I grabbed my phone and looked her up on Instagram. I scrolled through pic after pic. A lot of them were of her playing a piano. It made me wonder what she sounded like playing one of those after what I'd just heard. Some were of a giant black German Shepherd looking dog. Some were of her by the river. She always had some kind of instrument in her hand.

I finally came across a clip of her playing the piano.

I hit play and closed my eyes.

I listened to her voice—soft at first turning into a breathy whisper—and I couldn't recall hearing anything so breathtaking in my life. When the last key was played, I opened my eyes and then hit play again. This time I had to watch her while she performed. I wasn't a creep. Hell, I'd never even had a girlfriend. I mean, I had had a few dates, and while the girls I'd gone out with were, I dunno, pretty, I guess, they were as dull as a fifty-year-old butter knife, as Dad would say.

There was something about this girl, this bohemian, converse wearing, piano playing siren that had my head spinning.

I sat in the Burrito Bun parking lot well past sunset hitting play over and over again, thinking of Laurel Bennett and wondering how I'd never really noticed her before. I went to bed thinking about her and woke up hearing her voice in my head.

Looking back, it was no surprise I'd found my way back there on Main Street where she was busking the next evening.

The surprising part was after she was done playing and the crowd moved on, she'd asked me out for ice cream.

Chapter Two

The Dairy Duchess

Laurel

"When is Emily getting back from camp?" Dad asked.

"She still has another week," I answered, closing up my ukulele case.

"It's probably been pretty boring for you without her here, huh?"

"Nah. I'm trying to make some money, save up, so I've been busking every evening. At least that's my plan until Emily gets back," I said, grabbing my case, and phone, waiting for Dad to walk out the door, me following behind him.

Emily was my cousin, born a few days apart from me. We were more like best friends. I was homeschooled my entire life until I allowed Emily to talk me into starting freshman year with her at high school.

She didn't want to start out all alone and if I were being honest, at the time, I was curious how the other half lived. I knew it wasn't going to be anything like what the movies depicted, but still, there was no such thing as prom or homecoming when you were homeschooled.

Going into my senior year, I could honestly say upon reflection it was a mixed bag for me. There were pros and cons on both sides of the coin as my dad would say. Going to school certainly provided all kinds of opportunities to be around people, and well, sometimes being around people sucked. Being homeschooled also allowed for my parents to take me all over the place with them. What other kid could travel up and down the east coast doing art shows throughout the year?

It all came out in the wash, six of one and half a

dozen of another, as my dad would also say.

We were going down to The Infamous Art Gallery. It was this cool art collective where there were themed art exhibits monthly, open mics which I performed at, and they often would have some incredible jazz acts. They were pretty chill and would allow me to busk pretty much right at their front door. While I was doing that, Dad was between being outside watching and supporting me and being inside and part of that scene.

I'd had a decent crowd the evening before and was hoping for the same or a better one. Good weather was at least on my side. That meant people would be walking up and down the sidewalks.

Dad parked the truck and we both hopped down. He walked in the gallery. I sat outside on a large flower planter with enough seating for ten people, and room in front for passers-by to get a show.

It was odd to me—playing for an audience. As much as I felt at home with an instrument in my hands, the unnerving part of self-doubt always lingered on the fringes, and I had to fight to keep those feelings at bay.

I opened my ukulele case and withdrew the beautiful instrument my parents bought me as a birthday gift several years ago. Piano was my instrument of choice, but playing a piano was not exactly busking friendly.

I played a few Beatles tunes, and there were a few couples who stopped and listened. Some even threw a few dollars in my open case. But as I finished *Yesterday* by The Beatles and tore into a Patsy Cline song, the strangest thing happened.

The same guy who threw five dollars at me and practically ran away last evening came back.

As I played and sang, my gaze lingered where he was leaning up against the wall.

Brayden Anderson.

That was his name. I didn't have any classes with him, but I recognized him. I'd say we'd probably exchanged ten words between us over the last three years since I started at Buckhannon Upshur High School. That was until yesterday evening. And then I guess you could say we exchanged twenty words.

The curious part was that he came back again.

I didn't read too much into it, but I didn't think it was a mere coincidence that he happened to be walking down the street at the same exact time I was playing as I did yesterday.

Billie Jo came out, this cool chick who was also a member of the collective and sat a bottle of water down for me.

"Thank you," I mouthed.

She winked at me and snapped a few pics that I knew she'd post later on Facebook. Sigh. My dad's friends were the coolest.

As I wrapped up Patsy Cline, I was thinking of my next tune. I eyeballed my case. I could see from where I sat that I'd maybe earned twenty bucks. Not bad for thirty minutes.

I quickly downed half a bottle of water.

After sitting my water down, I looked up and saw that in addition to Brayden, there were a few older people still lingering.

"Any requests?" I asked my audience of three.

I was glad to be sitting down because you could've knocked me over with a feather when Brayden—this boy who I only knew well enough to know he was on the football team and he and I moved in entirely different circles—stepped forward in a hurry and didn't hesitate to speak up.

"Do you know *I'm So Lonesome I Could Cry* by

Hank Williams?" he asked while simultaneously blushing.

I was so stunned I couldn't answer. It felt like we held each other's gazes for an eternity. That song. That song of all the songs he requested...

If I'd had my fiddle, I would've done the song even better justice, but I didn't. What I had was my ukulele, my love for that exact song, and a perfect evening to belt out what was the anthem of my life.

When I sang it, I felt it deep in my bones and I meant every word.

Normally, I would keep my gaze focused on my instrument while playing, or look out into the audience, but never at anyone in particular. But there was something about this specific summer evening, being surrounded by the purple sky Hank always crooned about, and the boy in front of me hanging on every word I sang like I had the answers to the riddles that plagued his life, that made me keep my gaze fixed with his.

It was an odd connection. Odd and supernatural and spiritual all at the same time.

I didn't know what in the hell was going on between Brayden Anderson and I, or what Hank Williams had to do with it, but we were going to settle it over some ice cream.

This was what my dad would call a serendipitous moment.

Up until now, I'd never thought of Brayden. The only similarity we had was that we both attended the same high school. But that was literally it.

Until now.

He requested Hank Williams, and not just Hank Williams, but the song of my life.

I played and sang with all the soul the song deserved, never allowing my gaze to trail from his. And to Brayden's credit, he never flinched. He locked eyes with me and stayed right there in that moment with me.

It was as though everything else faded away and all there was was Brayden, me, and a song that was somehow weaving this untold story we had yet to discover.

I finished the last chord and rested my hand on the neck of my ukulele. I was spent and speechless. The few people that were around clapped, smiled, and placed tips in my case, and I knew this was going on around me, but I was fixed on Brayden.

He was the only thing I could see, and for some reason, it was as though I had never seen him before. He lit up just like in the song; he was illuminated.

Somewhere within, I dug deep and brought myself back to the present. I lowered my ukulele down into its home and looking briefly at the case, I remembered the evening before. Brayden threw five bucks in.

I don't know what made me do it—maybe post euphoria of singing my favorite Hank Williams song—but I closed my case and stood inches in front of Brayden. Just as bold as bold could be, I said, "You didn't get that sundae yesterday. How about we both go get one, on me?"

He looked surprised but was quick to respond. "Yeah, that sounds great." He smiled and God in heaven, up this close, I saw the smallest of dimples.

I picked up my case and quickly put it inside the door of the art gallery. We walked in silence and usually that would've been such an awkward thing to do, but for some reason this silence between us seemed natural.

The Dairy Duchess was literally within eyesight, so it took no time at all to get there. Walking up to the counter, I stole a sideways glance at him. He had a head full of thick brown hair that touched his shoulders, with dark blue eyes. He had kind eyes, eyes that made me feel there was a song in there somewhere waiting to be written.

"Ugh, I'd like a hot fudge sundae, medium," Brayden said, turning to me. "What would you like?"

Requesting Hank Williams and well mannered … I was intrigued. I couldn't wait to tell Emily about this, or maybe I could. I could hear her giggling and cracking jokes at my expense, which is exactly what I'd do to her.

"I think I'll have the same," I answered, pulling out the five-dollar bill from Brayden yesterday.

"Oh, ugh, I've got it," he said, struggling to spit the words out while jamming a hand into his pocket, likely digging around for cash.

"I know," I smiled. "This was for your ice cream yesterday, but you're buying both of ours today."

He only gave a sheepish smile, and it was oddly endearing.

What in the hell was happening?

I let my curiosity guide me. I was interested to know how Brayden came to be in the audience yesterday and this evening. I wondered how we both attended the same school together for the last three years and were complete strangers, and seemingly opposites. And I was curious how over hot fudge sundaes I instantly wanted to know everything about him.

Chapter Three

The Golden Hour

Brayden

"What classes are you taking this year?" Laurel asked, I think trying to lead me into conversation.

"Psychology with—"

"Mr. Carol," she said, finishing my sentence. "Gag."

"You don't like him?"

"I had him last year. Was pretty stoked to take his class, and he just failed epically."

"Oh yeah?"

"Mm-hmm," she said, swallowing down a spoonful of vanilla ice cream. "Lesson learned. Just because a teacher is somewhat around your age, or at least within a decade of your age, does *not* make them cool. Turns out, I *love* the eighty-year-old couple, Mr. and Mrs. McKenzie that substitute for everyone. I get to hear every morning the love story of how they met sixty years ago. Mr. McKenzie says they went to college together, and have worked together, basically been together every day for the last sixty some years. Can you imagine?" She stopped long enough to take another half-melted spoonful of sundae. "I love everything about them. I wish they taught full time. I love her cardigan sweaters with brooches, like who wears those anymore? Ya know?"

I didn't actually know what a brooch was, but I hung on every word she said.

"Her hot pink lipstick, the way Mr. McKenzie reminisces about how they met, how she's packed them both lunches all these years. They are more than adorable; they are like the god and goddess of teachers. They should be the standard, what everyone aspires to be."

"You mean to become teachers?" I asked, half smiling.

She laughed out loud, and I thought her singing was beautiful, but her laugh was warm and sincere. Something about that combination and me having been the one to induce it stirred something in me. I wanted to hear her laugh again and again.

"Yeah, the teaching part of that is absolutely what I was referring to," she said, finishing the last of her nearly melted sundae. "So, Brayden," she said, still with a coy smile on her face, "have you ever been to our open mic?"

"Oh, um, no," I answered, feeling like I dodged something uncomfortable.

"Oh. Hmm." She looked at me thoughtfully. "I'm curious about something."

Oh God. Here it was. The dreaded part where I was going to try to not sound stupid. I started shaking my leg under the concrete table—a nervous habit I couldn't remember not suffering from. Coach Westfall yelled at me in the locker room anytime he caught me shaking my leg, which was usually at half time if we were losing and he was chewing our butts out. His deep, bellowing voice had a way of making a person squirm.

"Tell me why you chose *I'm So Lonesome I Could Cry*?"

I didn't sit there that long before spitting out an answer, but it seemed to me like time was frozen momentarily while I clumsily contemplated how to approach an answer. How could I tell her why? Without sounding like a complete creep? I'd spent the last twenty minutes with her, but I spent the better part of last evening and today watching her music videos. While they were all incredible performances, there was one in particular, the one of her singing about robins and leaves and purple skies, that was, well, special. More than special. It was believable. It was vulnerable. It was eerie and haunting. It was soothing. It was aching. And I guess there was something in her sweet song that made me want to be the one to fix that pain she was singing about, ease the ache she so clearly felt, like I was some kind of hero in a teenage ballad.

In football when you're faced with a crossroad like I found myself in, you either had to punt and pray, or throw a Hail Mary and pray. Either way, you had to pray.

In this case, I just decided to tell her the truth. And pray.

"I heard you sing last night when I came walking down the sidewalk, and I guess I thought you sounded pretty good. So, I looked up your music and that song…" I scrubbed my face nervously with my open palm. "That song, was my favorite. I guess I wanted to hear it live." I looked straight at her. "From you." I couldn't sing to save my life, but I could be vulnerable, something else I didn't like, but there it was—all my insecurities laid out in front of her in the form of the simple truth for her to do with whatever she wanted. She could fling it back in my face, or call me a stalker, or better yet—tell all of her friends what I'd just confessed to her. God. I was dying inside of embarrassment.

But instead, she surprised me.

"Well, I was hoping you liked my music," she said, and I finally let out the breath I'd been holding, thankful that I somehow hadn't blown whatever this was between us.

"Oh yeah?"

"Yes," she answered, her lips curving up in a confident smile.

"Why's that?"

"Well, I saw you hearted every one of them, so I was hoping you meant it."

I'm pretty sure my face was red hot with embarrassment. I'm not sure why I had forgotten, but I guess I did hit the heart button on all her videos on Instagram. Good grief. Well, I had no game plans, no football film to study, no strategy. I was completely making this up as I went along.

Honesty. I was just going to let that guide me with Laurel and allow the chips to fall where they may, and maybe throw a couple Hail Marys.

"I did," I said, my voice soft, low. "I really did. I mean, I do."

Her smile fell just a little, but the sincere humor was still there. It was just that her smile, the expression in her eyes, seemed to be a bit more serious now. She looked down to my lap for a moment, and then back up to me. She leaned in a little closer across the table, just enough to grasp my hand in hers and give it a squeeze.

Her hand was as warm as her gaze. A gaze that looked like the living embodiment of that golden hour my mama went on and on about. I finally understood just how beautiful that could be.

Chapter Four

The Hand Never Forgets

Laurel

I'm not sure where I got my brazenness. My mother, I think. My dad was pretty reserved in that regard, as in I don't think in a million years he would've grabbed my mom's hand twenty minutes into a date. But according to her, and undisputed by my father, she kissed him on date number two. Now, I had no plans of *that*. But grabbing Brayden's hand … now that *was* something I was glad of.

I remembered the first time, even though years ago, my fingers glided across the keyboard of a piano. I also remembered the first time Dad rested a guitar in my lap and how the strings just seemed to navigate to the right fingertips. I also remembered the first time I played a fiddle. My hands knew and had a memory all of their own. And I guess like my German Shepherd, Zelda, just knew if you were made of good human stuff or bad, my fingers, my hands, they just knew if things were … *right*.

And when I grabbed Brayden's hand, he fit like a glove. He felt … right.

My parents believed me to have a unique condition—haptic memory, which means I can identify objects, know what they are, understand them so to speak, like say, an instrument simply by touching them. The unique part of this condition is that haptically acquired information is short lived as in the memory fades within seconds. For me, to date, my haptic memory has never faded. And my hands simply know if something or someone feels right.

I never forget.

My hand in Brayden's fit like a glove and felt like

that first key that hit my fingertip, that first guitar string, that first time I wrapped my hand around the neck of the fiddle.

I'm not sure why there was no awkwardness between us because the entirety of the situation should've been, but it simply wasn't there when I grabbed his hand, when he walked me back to the gallery, and not even when we gave each other our phones to plug in our numbers.

We left each other there, and even though Dad offered to let me drive to get in more practice, my mind was too busy thinking about the evening and too distracted thinking about Brayden to want to drive.

Dad knew something was on my mind as I absentmindedly looked out the window going down route twenty, but he never pushed me. And I was glad, because while the evening with Brayden felt right, that didn't mean I could explain it. All I knew was I wanted to explore more time with him.

Dad pulled into our driveway and our beautiful dog, Zelda, was there to meet us. Always happy, always like the first time she laid eyes on us and fell in love with her family. Zelda was ten, getting up in years for a German Shepherd, but she moved and acted like she was still two. Our youthful baby.

I scratched her between the ears, and she trailed in the house behind me.

"I'm going to work in the studio a bit tonight. I'm in the middle of a piece for the next show. I think you'll like it," Dad said, grabbing a bottle of water turning around to go right back out the door.

"In case I'm in bed before you get back in, goodnight and I love you," I said.

"Love you too."

I went to the stove to turn on the kettle. Some hot

tea with cream and sugar sounded like the perfect nightcap. In my way to make it, my phone dinged. Our service was horrid here, but occasionally if the wind didn't blow and the sky was clear and calm, texts would manage to come through.

Brayden: **do you like swimming**

Laurel: **Yes.**

Brayden: **me too**

Brayden: **Ugh...**

Maybe this was his idea of small talk?

Brayden: **wanna go with me**

Brayden: **Swimming???**

My face lifted in a smile as I leaned against the kitchen sink, Zelda leaning up against my bare leg. If we were still, she always had to lean into us, like touching us gave her security and peace of mind.

Laurel: **yeah**

Laurel: **I think that sounds fun. Yes.**

Brayden: **like noon**

Laurel: **Sure.**

Brayden: **how do I get to your house**

Well crap. I was going to have to tell Dad now. He was cool, but there was no way he was just going to let some boy come up here to our house and pick me up without meeting him first. Another thought flickered through my head, and I cringed. A swimming suit. Maybe I didn't think this through. I was trying not to panic as images of my glowing white legs smacked the front of my brain. Could you wear jogging pants? Was that acceptable?

Laurel: **Do you know where Czar is?**

Brayden: **Yeah**

Laurel: **Once you are in Czar, stay right after the turn where you have to yield and drive for about another five minutes and our house is the yellow one**

on the left with all the flowers.

Brayden: **i know the one**

Laurel: **Cool**

Brayden: **see you tomorrow**

I turned the hot water off as it spewed everywhere. "Oh, my gawd, Zelda. Do I cut off pants? I don't even think I have a bathing suit."

Zelda looked up at me like she understood everything I said. And I believed she did.

After fixing my tea and sipping on it, I wracked my brain on what to wear tomorrow. I went into the bedroom and started going through drawers, tossing out outfit after outfit like a racoon going through trash.

Zelda jumped up on my bed and watched the show.

I finally came across a pair of gray jogging pants. I laid them out on the bed and wasted no time cutting them and trying them on to see where the bottom landed.

"I don't know, girl, what do you think?" I asked, looking at Zelda, who tilted her head from side to side. "I know, but it's what I've got."

After hemming up the frays, I drifted off to sleep, thinking about swimming, Brayden, and the feel of his warm hand in mine.

"Night, Zelda."

****

I smelled the coffee Dad was making before I opened my eyes. Zelda had long since jumped off my bed, likely Dad let her out to use the bathroom. I stretched and yawned one last time before sitting up. I instantly recalled the last few evenings. Brayden. I smiled. I grabbed my phone to check the weather, hoping for a decent day.

High eighty-six, ten percent chance of rain, partly cloudy. Perfect.

I threw the covers off, put on my slippers, and met my dad in the kitchen.

"Good morning," he said, pouring coffee for both of us. I always looked up to the handcrafted wooden rack he made for my mother, her cup still dangled there, an equally handmade pottery cup from our favorite potter, unused. We all used to drink our coffee outside on the deck when it was warm, but when things change, so do some habits. It was now just me, Dad, and Zelda.

"Good morning," I said as he put his cup up to his lips to drink. "I think I have a date with a boy."

He choked on the hot coffee and spit a little bit into the sink. Wiping his mouth, face scrunched up, he said, "What?"

"His name is Brayden. We go to school together." Zelda leaned into me. I reached down, never breaking eye contact with my dad, and scratched her between the ears. She was so soft. Hopefully she had my back.

"No."

"What do you mean 'no'?"

"No. This is how it starts. Just *no*," Dad said, patting his shirt dry from where he spilled his coffee.

I sighed to myself. I knew I was going to have a bit of a hard time with this. "This is how what starts?"

"One date leads to another and then another, and then the next thing you know, he'll take you away from me. I just can't have it."

I smiled. I loved my dad. He was so overprotective. I knew he would be a little dramatic, well, *a lot* dramatic. Past that, he was simply the best father anyone could ask for. He'd allowed me all the creative freedom in the world. He encouraged my love of art, buying instruments when I knew often money was tight. Somehow, he managed to always keep me outfitted in the things I needed, and I loved him for all the struggles I could imagine he dealt with that I was unaware of. And the one that cut us both the deepest … the struggle to not only be Dad, but also be Mom. He never complained. Never.

"Dad, he's coming here at noon. He's really a nice boy. This is what kids my age do," I said gently. I knew I was going to have to be easy in guiding him into allowing me to go anywhere with a boy.

"What?" he said with all the shock of someone who'd just received the most unwelcome news.

****

"It's nice to meet you," Brayden said, jutting his hand out toward Dad. I could see he was a bit nervous.

I'd had a good three hours to get my dad prepped for this.

And it took all three of them.

"Laurel tells me you two go to school together," he said, shaking his hand back.

"Yes."

Zelda kept circling him and, to be honest, between my dad and my dog, Brayden never cracked, and Zelda never bit. Hmmm. Zelda always knew. She finally stopped circling him and in what felt very surprising and encouraging at the same time to me, I watched her sit beside him and lean into him. A definite sign from her that he was made of good stuff.

"So, Brayden," Dad began, and I got a bit nervous by the sound of his voice. "Where do you plan on taking my daughter?"

"Oh, swimming."

Crap. I hadn't told him that.

"Oh yeah?" Dad said, giving me a sideways glance.

"Yes, sir."

"Zelda, go get in the buggy."

I watched Zelda lose her mind, running in circles a few times, and then like she was that puppy again, she jumped into our side-by-side. As Zelda jumped, my heart dropped.

My dad had outsmarted me. "Let me show you the best spots around here to swim." My dad smiled from ear to ear.

Sigh. Well played.

SASHA HIBBS

Chapter Five

Ten Mile

Brayden

If I'd thought throwing money at Laurel the night she tried talking to me was awkward, sitting up front with her dad in their buggy riding to a swimming hole really took the cake. Their monster dog sniffed me all over for a solid two minutes before I guess deciding not to bite me. And even better, the dog was sitting in the back with Laurel instead of me. This wasn't exactly how I planned this out.

I didn't have much reason to be in Czar, but it was a pretty town. If you kept driving it would take you to Helvetia–a German-Swiss community where my dad always took my mom on Mother's Day. We would all go to the Hütte for their Sunday buffet once a year. I wondered briefly about taking Laurel there…

Riding in a side-by-side was always loud, which at least saved me from having to come up with conversation with her dad, but not for long as we pulled down onto a gravel road that soon gave way to a large swimming hole.

As he parked, their dog, Zelda, hopped out and went straight for the water.

"Here's as good a spot as any," her dad said, as he grabbed a few camp chairs from the back.

Laurel had a towel in one hand and a small case in the other. She walked up to me a bit sheepishly and whispered where only I could hear her, "Sorry. He ambushed me."

"Nah. It's cool," I whispered back to her. This close, I could see the small flecks of what looked like rust spots speckled across hazel-colored irises. It was a very interesting color. Conscious that her dad was likely watching every move, I started walking toward the swimming hole.

This wasn't exactly what I'd anticipated, but I was going to go along to get along.

"Have you ever been here before?" her dad asked.

"I don't think so."

"Where do you live?"

"About ten minutes outside of Buckhannon, going toward Hodgesville." I was hoping there weren't too many more questions coming my way.

"Do you see those large bushes over there?"

"The mountain laurel?" I said.

His face softened a bit. "Yes, exactly." He seemed somewhat impressed that I recognized the plant. "Laurel was named after them. They were her mother's favorite flowers, at least when in bloom."

Although the time had passed to see the clusters of star-like white flowers, I knew them well.

I heard her before I saw her. A sweet, eerie tune came from behind me. Instantly, I relaxed, even with her father watching. Her music, her voice, it, no, *she*, just had a way to make my muscles go weak, so I'd found out over the course of forty-eight hours. When I turned, I was struck by how pretty she was. She sat perched on a large river rock, her now wet dog laying at her feet, and the sun hitting them both made the scene in front of me look like an album cover my mom would've had from the nineties, Fiona somebody. I felt terrible I couldn't remember because it was her favorite singer.

She smiled at me, but it was a mischievous smile. I wondered if she started singing to distract her father's questioning of me.

I couldn't help but smile back at her.

I slowly waded into the water. It was cool, but with it so hot out it felt perfect.

She wrapped up singing, which I was disappointed in, mainly because I loved to hear her voice. Secondly because it provided a great excuse to avoid talking to her dad who I didn't know and had no clue what to talk about. Honestly, I really didn't know Laurel, but the desire to know her better was what made me put up with all of this.

Laurel waded in the water shortly after I did, her dog, Zelda, right behind her. Her dad stayed on the bank, but he could see everything easily. I really didn't know what to say or do. This was a bit weird but worth it. Especially thinking of Laurel's music.

"Dad." Laurel looked at me briefly before looking over to her dad. "I don't think I told you that Brayden plays football, or he's on the football team, I mean to say. Or I guess he plays football and is on the team, like I guess you can do both." She was getting flustered, and I felt her pain. I smiled inside that she was perhaps getting flustered on my behalf.

"Oh yeah?"

"Yeah. I play safety."

"Safety. Sweet. Who's your team?"

Oh God. This was what could make or break me. I was at least thankful for the cold water masking the fact I was sweating. I rolled the dice. "The Steelers."

I slowly exhaled the breath I was holding as I watched her dad smile from ear to ear. "Laurel, you may have hit the jackpot yet."

"Oh God, Dad," Laurel murmured under her breath, her face red hot with embarrassment.

"Oh, calm down," he said, waving her off. "We are Steelers fans around here. My wife and I are from Uniontown, Pennsylvania. I grew up in Steelers country.

Laurel here was born during the 2005-2006 Super Bowl where the Steelers won. That girl has brought me nothing but luck since."

"That entire era of Steeler football was pretty epic. Polamalu was probably my favorite," I said, feeling a little more comfortable. I could talk football. I loved football. And thank God, it would appear Laurel's dad did too.

Her dad skipped a rock across the water, and I watched the ripple effect the rock produced. Wading in that cold water, that hot August day all those months ago, I was a clueless boy who, like that rock skipped across water, had no idea how profound and severe rippling effects could have.

****

After piling back into the buggy, we headed back to her house. It was not the worst way to spend a day. A bit strange, was more like it, which honestly, Laurel and her dad both seemed a bit odd. I heard her dad mention that his wife was from Pennsylvania, but nothing more about her. We pulled into her driveway and after getting out, before leaving Laurel and I alone, her dad turned to me and said in a polite but very serious tone to where only I could hear, "I suppose any boy who is willing to go on a first date of sorts with the dad *and* talk football is good enough to date my girl. Be careful though, aside from Zelda, she's the only girl I got."

Fair enough, I thought to myself.

"I'll be in the studio if you need me."

I watched her dad turn and trail off into a large red studio across from their house.

Zelda remained behind. Interestingly enough, she padded over, sat right beside me, and leaned into my leg.

"Wow. She likes you," Laurel said. "She doesn't do that with everybody. She'll want you to scratch between her ears."

I looked down into a pair of soft, intelligent brown eyes. I bent over and gently scratched her between the ears. She leaned even further into me. I could easily understand how someone would be a dog person.

"I'm sorry Dad surprised you like that. He surprised me too," she said, and I could hear the smallest trace of nerves in her voice.

"Really, it's fine. I don't mind," I said, trying to encourage her. My mind briefly flickered to what her dad said moments ago, about being able to date Laurel, perhaps without him present. We'd have to try this again. Minus her dad. What would that look like? I had no experience in dating. I was making this up as I went.

"Do you like hot dogs?" she asked.

"Yeah."

"Are you hungry?"

Once she said it, I became pretty fixated on it. "Very."

"Great. Follow me."

Zelda got up and followed Laurel, as did I. We went into her house. I kind of followed her lead. She was in the kitchen gathering stuff up, and I was trying not to let my eyes roam too much.

"We can go up to the fire pit and roast hot dogs," she said, throwing a pack of hot dogs, buns, ketchup, and mustard into a small basket.

"Can I help?"

"Uh, sure. You grab this and I'll grab my guitar."

I felt my heart race a little at the thought of hearing her play so intimately. I took the basket from her and stood by the door while she vanished into what I presumed to be her bedroom momentarily before emerging with a guitar in hand.

After opening the door for her, I followed behind

her, walking up this gorgeous path where there was nothing but ferns and moss on either side. We didn't go far before stopping at what looked like a fire pit with a few chairs sitting around.

I looked around to see where there might be twigs to start a fire. I set the basket down on a stainless-steel table near the pit.

She rested her guitar gently against one of the chairs while Zelda laid down at the foot of one. "We need some kindling," Laurel said. "How about I gather up some while you sharpen a few roasting sticks?"

"Sure. Sounds like something I could do," I said, looking behind me, scouring for two sturdy sticks. After finding what I believed to be good candidates, I pulled out my pocketknife, something I had to practice taking out of my pocket every night so I wouldn't accidentally take it into school. I whittled the ends of two sticks until I felt pretty sure they would hold hot dogs.

Laurel was busy throwing small pieces of kindling into the pit and stacking it in such a way that air would easily fan the fire. I could tell by the way she stacked the sticks, someone with experience showed her how to build a great fire. I was about to offer my help when I saw that she clearly didn't need it.

After wadding up a few newspapers and placing them under the stack of kindling, Laurel lit the ends and it wasn't a minute later, the kindling erupted in fire.

Impressive.

Laurel had the voice of an angel.

She could build a fire better than me.

Eating my hot dog, watching her perch herself up on a river rock covered in moss with the occasional ray of sunshine bursting through down on her, and hearing her croon about broken hearts and eternal love, I couldn't imagine feeling more … complete.

THE TRUTH ABOUT FIREFLIES

Laurel was pure joy.

Looking back, I can see just how easy I fell, and how I would come to empathize with the brokenhearted bastards she sang about, and just how little I knew.

SASHA HIBBS

Chapter Six

The Kids Are All Right

Laurel

"He seems all right, I guess," Dad said, varnishing one of his latest paintings outside while I sat in my favorite wicker chair with a cup of evening tea in one hand and Zelda at my feet.

"You guess?" I said, verbally poking at him. I really wasn't sure what to think of Brayden. The entire situation was bizarre, new, and frustrating all at the same time.

"Well, I suppose any boy that can withstand a parental hijacking on their first date is okay. He didn't jump in his truck the minute we got back here either."

I laughed at him. I loved my dad. It had just been him and I these last couple of years. Well, him, I, and Zelda. We had to adjust after Mom… The lump forming in my throat at the thought of her made me stop. Some things were just too painful. Her absence was one of them. I cleared my throat. "What's the theme this month?"

"For the Birds!"

I could've figured as much. Ever the funny guy, he'd painted a portrait of a bird in a dress with antique-looking wallpaper as a backdrop.

"It looks like you're ready at least."

"Somehow I got mine done a few weeks before instead of the day of."

"I'm impressed," I said, taking the painting in. Mom would've thought it funny and beautiful at the same time. Anything Dad painted, sculpted, forged, period … she always wanted to keep.

"Few more weeks before the start of school.

Senior year," Dad said, in a reminiscent tone. "How did that happen?"

"What? Me getting to my senior year? Well, I hope it's because you've raised an intelligent kiddo, mister." I smiled.

"Ha. Ha. Time, Laurel. Where did the time go?" He sat the painting down and I had to be careful his mood didn't take a turn. "I thought I had more time."

"I don't know about time, but I do know about me," I said, sitting forward. "You will always have me." I was going to have to change the topic because my dad was fast approaching what they call empty nest syndrome and if this is how he felt with an entire year left with me, it was going to be even harder on him after. And I didn't want that for Dad. I wanted him to be happy. He'd always been the best father in the world to me.

"Emily will be back soon. I have so much catching up to do with her. Did you eat the hot dogs I made you?"

"No. I was busy with this and wanted to get it finished while I was feeling up to it," he said looking at his work. Dad always said the artist thing wasn't something you could force. You either felt it or you didn't, and if you tried pushing yourself it would reflect in the work. So, he would always strike while the proverbial iron was hot.

"Well, then. You can eat now." I sat my cup of tea down and went in to heat up his supper. My phone started dinging once I walked in.

While the microwave was on, I pulled my phone out and opened up my messages.

Brayden.

Strange, but I liked that he was messaging me.

I took Dad out his hot dogs and made up an excuse to go back inside. I pulled my phone out to look at the messages.

Brayden: **i really liked the hot dogs**

Laurel: **Well, I've been told I can make a mean dog.**

I smiled.

Brayden: **you buy ice cream, make incredible hot dogs and sing your face off**

This was followed by several laugh emojis.

I had a thought. Normally, I'd be pretty nervous about performing so privately. It was one thing to play for an audience that you could distantly connect with, but another to be playing for one single individual. A bit unnerving, really. But somehow, Brayden didn't bother me.

Laurel: **What are you doing tomorrow?**

Brayden: **i have football practice at noon then nothin**

Laurel: **Cool.**

Brayden: **any reason???**

Laurel: **Maybe ....**

Brayden: **???**

Laurel: **You free tomorrow evening?**

Brayden: **yeah**

Laurel: **Meet me at The Dairy Duchess around 5.**

He sent a thumbs up emoji followed by another smiley face emoji. He must have a thing for those.

****

I'm not sure what I expected ... him to be sweaty after football practice? Instead, he showed up showered and smelling like fresh linen.

"How about ice cream and a show?" I asked.

"I'm in," he answered promptly, and I found it cute, that assertive yet shy confidence.

"Well, then, you are in for a real treat." I smiled.

"Ready to order?"

"Oh, yeah," he said, almost sheepishly, like I caught him doing something he wasn't supposed to be doing, or as though I could hear his thoughts.

"Two hot fudge sundaes," he ordered at the window. Turning quickly, almost panicked, he said, "Are you okay with a hot fudge sundae?"

"Oh, yeah, sure. Fine with me." I watched him relax his shoulders, relieved.

We downed our sundaes and before he had time to do or say anything, I led with, "Follow me."

"Are we driving?" he asked.

"Well, I'm not driving anywhere. I don't have my license yet. Late bloomer, I guess. I do have my permit, but to answer your question, no. We can walk."

He seemed curious and confused, but after throwing our trash away, he fell into sync beside me without question.

"This show doesn't cost any money. Plus, I'm trying to save up for a car. Anything I make, Dad will match."

"What kind of car?" he asked, sweeping his long bangs away from his eyes as he looked over at me.

"Easy. I want a 2005 Subaru Outback. I love those old wagons."

"Makes sense. They go great in the snow."

"Ugh, snow. I hate the cold. I hate snow and dreary gray days. Blah."

"So, you don't want a Subaru because of the all-wheel drive?" he asked, a bit confused.

"I mean, I guess that's definitely a bonus, but for me I like the style of them, and it was the kind of car I can first remember my parents having. A green limited-edition Outback. And I've wanted one ever since."

We continued walking down Florida Street toward

the college. He probably thought I was taking him to the theater on campus, but I was taking him somewhere else entirely.

We arrived at the steps of Herbert Hall, one of the many halls the college allowed the community to use for practice. There were already a few kids waiting for me.

"Hey, Ashley, Jackson," I said, waving. I knew a few more kids would trickle in, but these two were my youngest students, aged seven and eight. "We will be done by 6:30 PM," I said to their parents. "You all are welcome to stick around or swing back by."

I glanced over quickly to Brayden to assess his reaction. He was, for the most part, unreadable.

"Ready for the show?" I asked, smiling.

Hands in his pockets, a subtle yet definitely there smile, Brayden said, "Lead the way."

In total, I had four kids that I taught piano to for free.

We practiced some easy keys, and I praised their advancement. Brayden sat quietly observing from the front row. I could occasionally see one or two of my students eyeing him up curiously, but to their credit, they were on their best behavior.

"Great job, guys and gals! Now remember what we've learned this week, practice on the keyboards I sent you home with, and next week we will try an actual song from beginning to end."

There were a few groans mixed in with a few excited squeals. Parents started shuffling through, collecting their kids, leaving with a reminder to practice, practice, practice.

I was soon alone with Brayden. He sat in the front row looking up at me. I smiled and sat down at the familiar piano bench. I stretched my fingers, closed my eyes, and allowed the memory of my touch to take my hands on a journey they'd been on many times. I sang an old Irish jig about love in the midst of poverty, a song that always reminded me of my parents. We'd been various degrees of poor over my lifetime, but that never altered the mighty, mighty love between my parents nor me not realizing we were poor. I felt like the richest kid on the planet.

As I stroked the last note, I rested my palms over the keys, looking up at him. He was leaning forward in his chair, hands clasped in fists, resting against lips, obscuring his expression. He seemed interested, but I couldn't really tell what was going on in his head.

I closed the lid and stood up. The silence was beginning to make me feel a bit stupid when Brayden finally decided to speak up. "So, you offer these classes for free?"

I tucked a loose strand of hair behind my ear. "Oh, yeah. To these kids, I do."

"But aren't you trying to save up for a car?"

"Yeah, but these kids, these kids are so special and have nothing. At least in the financial sense. They have wonderful parents, good home lives, and while that is the most important, their parents don't have money to put them in extracurricular activities. So, I do what I can for those that are interested."

Brayden stood up. He looked over his shoulder, and then turned around as though taking the entirety of the music room in before looking back to me. If he thought me teaching a bunch of cute, deserving kids piano lessons for free was stupid, I would throat punch him. I took a few angry steps toward him. The elitist-football-playing-truck-that-his-parents-probably-bought-him-spoiled-brat had another thing coming.

"Laurel," Brayden said abruptly.

I felt my face get red with anger, and then quickly

change to embarrassment.

"My family is having a low-key cookout tomorrow. There's only going to be a few people over. My brother is in from college, so he will be there. Of course, my mom and dad, and an aunt and uncle. Would you, er, can I come pick you up around six?"

My hands were never wrong. He was warm. Brayden was warm. The hands always knew. The hands always knew.

SASHA HIBBS

Chapter Seven

Going Into Battle

Brayden

In life, there is that locker room pep talk you get from your coach, that one that lifts you up and makes you go from losing in the first half to coming back against all odds and winning in the second half, because well, you just got the most motivational speech you've ever heard in your life and you can't let your coach down. You can't let your teammates down. Those words somehow penetrate the fabric of your lifeblood and burns you from the inside out. Winning is the only option.

That was what listening to Laurel was like.

Moving.

She *moved* me.

I mean, I enjoyed music just like the next person, but until I met Laurel, I didn't know that there was more involved with music other than listening. I never exactly watched *and* listened. And if that wasn't enough, she reached kids with her ability. She selflessly devoted her time and gave others, who otherwise might not have the opportunity, a chance at learning something, something, something … meaningful.

That was Laurel, the living embodiment of that locker room speech. I'd never really thought of myself as a dickhead or a selfish person, but I also never really gave a ton of consideration to others.

As I sat back watching Laurel work with kids whose enthusiasm was almost tangible, I didn't know how to describe what I felt other than being … moved.

She seemed a bit taken aback, maybe even sidetracked when I asked her about coming to our cookout. But thankfully she agreed. I walked her back up to the gallery, and we parted ways with the understanding I would come pick her up tomorrow.

I drove home not even concerned about telling my parents about asking Laurel over. Instead, I found myself driving down Route 20, window down, breeze blowing, music blaring, sun hitting my face, and I guess enough giddiness that rather than keeping this to myself, I actually wanted to tell my parents about Laurel. I wanted them to meet her. How had I not noticed her before? She seemed to be all I could concentrate on now.

I pulled in the driveway and turned the engine off. Caleb, my older brother by two years, was in from Marshall University for the summer but was getting ready to go back in a few weeks to start the fall semester. His VW Beetle was parked beside my parents' Toyota RAV4.

The golden hour was approaching. I knew I'd find my parents in the back, specifically because it offered the best view of the sunset. I walked past the flower beds and around the house to the back patio where sure enough both my parents were sitting.

"I thought I heard you pull into the driveway," Mom said, looking at me sideways momentarily and then back in the direction of the setting sun.

"How was Ohio?" I asked, lowering myself down into a chair.

"Flat," Dad said with a half-smile. "How's practice been going? Coach killing you boys yet?"

"It's not been too bad," I said absently. "I'm bringing a friend over tomorrow, is that okay?" I decided to cut right to the chase.

"Like, friend, as in Chase?" Mom asked.

"Like a friend I go to school with and is also a girl."

My mom was a pretty happy person under any circumstance, but I swear when she heard this, I couldn't imagine ever seeing a bigger smile on her face in my entire life. If fireworks were a face, my mom's lit up like the fourth of July.

"Well. A girl, you say?" Dad said, wiggling his eyebrows. "Hey, hey."

"Her name is Laurel."

"Oh, honey! That's wonderful! A girl! Did you hear that, Matt? Brayden has a girlfriend he's bringing to the cookout," Mom said, starting to go into full party planning mode. "Do you know if there's anything in particular she likes? I'll have to run to the store. Maybe get something a little extra—"

"Mom, please. She's not exactly my girlfriend," I said with a bit of dread that my mom was already ready to plan our homecoming and prom pictures, and who knows, maybe she wouldn't stop there? Maybe she'd try planning out the rest of our lives.

"Oh, I understand, honey. I'll calm down. But how exciting!" She went back and forth between talking herself off the ledge and throwing herself into full on excitement. "Oh, her name is Laurel, Laurel what?" Mom asked, as though this important missing piece of information somehow brought her down from cloud nine back to planet earth.

"Laurel Bennett."

My parents looked at each other briefly before turning their gaze back to me.

"What?" I asked. My eyebrows scrunched up to match the confusion I felt. "Do you know her?"

Dad remained silent.

Mom's face softened. "No, not exactly. We know her parents." It was all she said with a forced smile, but I didn't understand why.

"Know her parents?" I repeated.

"Well, her mother has since passed, but let's not

let things turn grim. I'm very happy you are bringing her over."

****

Laurel was unlike any girl I'd ever met, or really what I should say, unlike any girl I'd ever noticed before. She hopped up into my truck, waving bye to her dad as we pulled out of her driveway and onto the main road in Czar. My gaze was firmly fixed on the road, but I could see her in my periphery looking all around the truck until she picked up a few CDs.

"Oh sweet! You've got CDs," she said, flipping them over and reading the back jacket. "I hate that everything is so new and now cars don't come with CD players. My parents met and married in the nineties, so that's all I grew up with. Well, CDs, vinyl, radio, and live music."

"Yeah, those were in here when I bought this," I said, glancing over at her real quick and then back to the road.

She popped one open and pushed it in the player.

"Guns N' Roses," she said, smiling, like she'd come across an old familiar friend. And then she began singing along, head bobbing, arms up like she was at a concert.

I was absolutely captivated.

Captivated by this carefree girl who had the voice and playing chops of some otherworldly creature, this happy go lucky live in the moment attitude. I glanced over from time to time, not taking my eyes off the road too long. It was hard to look at anything else but how the sun hit her hair, the movement of her body even while sitting down, the total lack of caring for what she was doing in front of others. She had everything going for her, and it made my chest *warm*. It was kind of like when you're cold and take a big drink of hot chocolate and it's the best sensation ever. That was her.

A few songs later and we pulled into my driveway. I could see everyone was here—Uncle Carl, Aunt Jennifer, Mom, Dad, and Caleb.

"I hope you like hamburgers," I said, turning the engine off.

"Who doesn't?" she said with a coy smile. "I tried the pescatarian lifestyle and we didn't work out too well."

I had to give her credit, if she was nervous, you'd never know. I was nervous going to her house and then dealing with her dad, who I'm sure was overbearing maybe because Laurel was his only daughter, or I don't know … maybe that was just the normal way dads acted with their daughters.

But not her. She had an easy manner about her with everyone. She seemed to be a natural at everything. Did she have any weaknesses?

As we rounded the corner to go to my backyard, I did the most impulsive thing I've done in my life, even more impulsive than throwing money at Laurel for busking and coming back the next night hoping to run into her.

I grabbed her hand.

I grabbed her hand so my family could see. I wanted them to see me holding her hand. But more importantly, *I* wanted to hold her hand.

Laurel never jerked away, didn't seem surprised, rather she surprised me by squeezing my hand back and turning the corner with me like we'd always been an item. I couldn't remember feeling happier.

To my family's credit, and maybe I owed thanks to divine intervention, no one said anything about our public display of affection. I was the most worried about Caleb, but unbelievably, he showed me mercy. Maybe college had matured him. I didn't know.

"Hey, everyone. This is Laurel," I said, turning toward her and then back to what felt like a thousand sets of eyes staring at us. "And this is my mom and dad, Aunt Jennifer, Uncle Carl, and my brother, Caleb."

With her free hand, she gave a polite wave. "Hi."

"Well, you two are just in time. The food is fresh off the grill," Mom said. A look passed between Mom and Laurel, one of recognition. It was odd. But this wasn't the time or place.

Today was about listening to vintage CDs while driving down the road, eating the best food with family, and feeling light as air, like a feather floating in the wind because Laurel had a way of making things feel weightless. She was doing things to me, like changing my internal structure. And I wanted more.

"You're a senior this year too?" Dad asked Laurel.

"Yes," she answered.

Mom was serving burgers to everyone.

"Do you have any plans after graduation?"

I was dipping out baked beans while Aunt Jennifer was busy pouring lemonade for everyone.

"Somewhat. I've been thinking about trying to get into some music programs," she said, taking the glass Aunt Jennifer offered.

"Laurel plays a lot of instruments," I said, sounding like an idiot.

"That's pretty cool," Mom said, sitting down to the table after serving burgers to everyone. "What's your preference?"

"The piano."

"Oh. So, you're looking at somewhere like Julliard," Caleb piped up while choking down a bite of hamburger.

"Ugh, yeah. Perhaps," Laurel answered, looking over at me quickly and then back to her food.

My dad had his own construction business and while he didn't expect me to stick around and take up the family business, I felt it was my obligation after Caleb bailed on it. I never even considered college because I was the only son left to live out my father's dream.

There was this one football game I regretted. We were up by one, the other team was on the ropes, it was fourth down, and all we had to do was stop them from getting the first down. The other team snapped the ball, and our defense read the play. The linebacker came in, hit the quarterback on the drop back, and knocked the ball loose on a strip sack. There the ball was, laying on the turf. The game was over essentially. All we had to do was fall on it. But all I could see was green in front of me. I picked that ball up and I ran.

I scored a touchdown.

But there was no cheering as our field goal unit came out onto the field to kick the extra point. A bad snap resulted in the kicker shanking the field goal. I'd just given the other team an opportunity to win.

There was only silence from the crowd holding their breath in fear, my teammates looking at me like, "What did you do?" Coach Westfall looked at me with absolute disappointment in his eyes.

And that was when I realized, I'd left the other team a chance. The only one they needed.

The other team got the ball back. But they didn't just get the ball back. When we kicked it off to them, they returned it for a touchdown, and they also nailed the two-point conversion, and they won.

Slow and steady wins the race. Coach always said that to us, like it was his motto. All we had to do was eat the clock. Stay in bounds and get tackled, eat the clock.

Slow and steady. But I blew the game then and much like that horrific Friday night on the field, I blew it with Laurel because I wasn't willing to go slow and steady. But this time it cost me more than a football game.

It would cost me her.

Chapter Eight

Open Mic

Laurel

"Brayden Anderson?" Emily said, her face scrunched up half in consideration and half in shock as she digested what I was telling her.

"Yep. Brayden. Anderson." Zelda sat leaning up against my one dangling leg from the wicker chair outside on my deck.

Emily got back in from camp last evening and of course if her grandfather would've let her, she'd have been at my house in an instant, but he wanted to spend the evening with her. After his wife died, it was just the two of them and he was lonely.

"How? I mean, why? No, I mean, how?"

I laughed. I knew this would be interesting to explain to Emily. "I already told you. My evil plan is working. He was put under my spell, and I now control him, and then soon the universe will be mine! Muahaha!"

"Huh, Brayden. I just never would've thought," Emily said, lightening up a little, but still trailing off in thought.

"I know, right?" I bent over and scratched Zelda between the ears, and I could tell she was content. "I mean, don't get me wrong, we've only been out a few times."

"He took you to his parents' house. For. A. Cookout," Emily said matter-of-factly. "I mean, this is like Romeo and Juliet shit."

"What?" I said, laughing at her.

"Oh, come on. Fall madly in love after one week."

"Whatever," I said, still laughing at her nonsense. "We are not madly in love, or any other kind of love, and we are not thirteen and sixteen, or whatever ridiculous age they were when they made their even more ridiculous decisions."

"Hey, they had to act fast. Back in those days, they didn't live past twenty-five," Emily said seriously. "There was no time to waste!"

"You are so funny," I said, giving her an eye roll. "I missed you."

Emily was my cousin—my dad's sister's daughter. Unfortunately, Emily's parents were not in the picture. A combination of drugs and jail left her in the custody of her grandfather, her dad's dad. Her grandfather, John, was nice enough, but I knew there were times Emily, like me, suffered for her missing mother. We relied on each other. And I loved her. With only a few months difference between us, Emily was more like my sister than anything.

"Two weeks left before school starts. How is this going to shake out?" Emily asked, a bit of mischievousness in her voice.

"What do you mean?

"Well, like what's going back to school this year going to look like?" Emily said, leaning in closer, eyebrow arched.

"Fair question. I think it's going to look a lot like junior year, but now we are seniors. I'm guessing they didn't do much redecorating wise to the school, maybe just some general touch up paint. Oh, the lockers! Now, I remember reading an article where they budgeted for new lockers they were going to install over the summer. So those should look new."

"Oh, very funny," Emily said, now giving me the eye roll. "I mean, do you think Brayden will come pick you up in the mornings before school?"

I hadn't really given any consideration to that possibility, but it seemed extremely far for a morning commute. "Um, I don't know. I wasn't planning on asking him. How was camp? Anything new happen? Did you meet anyone?"

"No, but nice way to change the subject," Emily said with a smirk. "Same boring shit. I only go because Pap thinks I like it."

"I know."

"Laurel Anderson," Emily said, changing gears. "It kinda has a ring to it." She smiled while wiggling her eyebrows at me.

I threw the pillow off the back of my chair at her.

She threw her hands up, dodging said pillow, while simultaneously squealing.

"You'll have to be on your best behavior. Please, promise me," I said, still smiling. "Open mic is tonight, and I think he's coming."

"I promise," she said, holding up her hand as though that made her promise somehow official and believable. It would have to be good enough for me.

****

There was a decent sized crowd. Open mic was my tribe, my people. Being homeschooled, my parents had taken me around all over the state to play at open mics. Playing in front of strangers wasn't an issue for me, nor was enjoying watching others get up on the stage and give a piece of themselves. School was both rewarding and frustrating in the music arena. I was used to being a solo act. Going to school and making the cut for their 'elite' choir taught me how to work musically as a team, but it was different, and still a bit hard three years later only because of having been a solo act since I came out of my mother's womb.

"Oh! The Pied Piper is here!" Emily whispered excitedly beside me.

My gaze followed the line of hers to where he was sitting.

The Pied Piper was this cool older gentleman who was always dapper looking with his feather capped fedora and checkered pants. He played a variety of wind instruments. At a glance, it was a bit of a struggle to take him seriously. But then he'd raise the flute up to his lips and blow you away.

"He's pretty awesome," I said in agreement. "And my favorite, *Revival Guns* is here too."

"Wonder where Brayden is?" Emily whispered.

"Who knows?" I said, nonchalantly, but I was wondering silently to myself that same thing, trying not to look or feel disappointed.

"Okay, folks. It's seven o'clock! Time to get open mic rollin'," The MC said from the stage. "First up, Wild Bill."

A round of applause erupted.

Wild Bill was a great old country act, usually playing covers of Willie Nelson, Merle Haggard, or Waylon Jennings accompanied by a banjo or dobro.

After Wild Bill played three songs, the MC got up and announced The Pied Piper, who was on point as usual. He finished playing his set and there was still no sign of Brayden. Maybe he'd bailed. I thought Emily may've thought the same, because instead of taking the opportunity to jab me and tease me more about him, she grew silent.

My favorite band took the stage—a local rockabilly group—that never failed to blow the doors off the hinges. People were screaming, clapping, dancing, and making spectacles of themselves, but that was okay here. You really couldn't get by with something like this in school—things were a bit more polished, but this, *this* was home to me and a safe space.

After the usual three song set of several acts going on coupled with some killer poetry readings, I was called up. The last to play.

"And closing our show tonight is none other than seventeen-year-old, Laurel Bennett! Always worth the ticket price."

It always cracked me up when the MC gave my introduction. I mean, there were no tickets. Open mic was free. But he had a sense of humor, and I knew it was just his way of engaging with the crowd.

Brayden never made it. I really didn't want to think too much about it, but at the same time I'd be lying if I said I didn't feel jilted in some way. He said he'd be here and after taking me to his parents' house, I felt we were heading in a direction that wasn't quite boyfriend and girlfriend declaration worthy yet, but something, some strange connection that if my hand could talk, it would describe that feeling, that warmth that said he was safe, he was real, he was something more, something *else*.

I carried on like nothing was wrong because as they say, the show must go on.

I sat down, determined to play some of my original music. Ideally, I'd play the piano, but in what seemed stupid now, I'd paid a little closer attention to what I wore and maybe added a little bit of make-up and thought the piano would obscure me from his sight.

I thought sitting up on the stage with my ukulele would have me seen at the best advantage. Lord, that was what I got for a small twinge of vanity that seemed to grow overnight.

I opened my case and withdrew my battle ax. Stretching my fingers, I wrapped them around the neck. I leaned into the microphone, closed my eyes, and the world melted away.

When I opened my eyes, the figure standing in the doorway, hovering like he was unsure of himself, caught my eye. I felt my face lift in a smile as our eyes met. I definitely had two songs left in me.

As I sang my heart out, I had a thought that seemed to work its way through my performance to the front of my mind.

Turned out, Brayden Anderson hadn't stood me up after all.

Chapter Nine

Pineapples, Pizza, and Pondering
Brayden

It seemed a bit surreal that after what felt like an eternity, senior year was practically here. This would be my last season playing football. I started playing, or was recruited I should say, in middle school. Our middle school coach saw something in me and I'd been playing ever since.

It was so hot I could see the haze. Coach didn't cut us any slack. He only screamed at us to hydrate more.

"Where in the hell have you been?" On my left, Chase was bent over ready to run beside me.

"What do you mean?"

"I mean where have you been the last couple of weeks?"

"I haven't missed practice."

Just then, the ball went flying and Chase and I both took off running, ready to tackle teammates standing in for offense. Practice was always weird to me. It was hard to pretend your teammates were the opposing team. It made tackling them harder to do, but Coach screamed at us if we hesitated, so, well, we didn't.

After Chase tackled Tate and they both got to their feet, I readjusted my gear in enough time for round two with Chase.

"No shit you've been coming to practice. That's not what I mean. Where. Have. You. Been?"

I wasn't keeping Laurel a secret by any means. Actually, I hadn't really even given any thought to discussing her with anyone but my parents. I guess I had been too busy going to open mic, or The Dairy Duchess, or anywhere really, to think about what I would've done with my time had I not heard her that night on the street. There'd been plenty of opportunities for mutual acquaintances to see us out, or my friends, but I guess for whatever reason, it just never happened.

Guys could be stupid, and I never really thought about what that meant until I had a girl to consider. Some jerks would talk about scoring with a girl, but now that I was thinking about it, none of the guys I'd grown up with, friends or not, ever discussed just a relationship with a girl. Period. Did the lack of conversation about dating, I mean seriously dating, mean that it was, well, serious?

"You've not—" Chase stopped short, his eyes grew big, and the look of him having an epiphany washed all over his face. "Ermahgerd. You're seeing a girl."

I wiped the sweat off my brow and looked over at him with a guilty as charged smile.

"Who is she?" he asked while stretching long, getting ready for the next snap. "No, don't tell me. Let me guess." He looked thoughtful for a moment before launching out a full list of names. "Is it Jessica? Mya? No, not Mya. Oh, I know. It's Raelynn. That girl's had a crush on you since kindergarten."

I shook my head at him and smiled. "No."

"Come on, man. Who is it?"

"Look out!" I yelled, as our feet flew over the field, soil flying in bits and chunks from our cleats.

Chase was too busy running his mouth and he missed the tackle. Coach threw his hat off while screaming, "Dammit, Heffinger! Get your ass in the game!"

"Sorry, Coach!" Chase yelled back while wiping debris off his shirt.

"Laurel Bennett," I said.

"Laurel Bennett? Homeschooled Laurel Bennett?" Chase repeated in a confused, trying to comprehend what I was saying, kind of way.

"Yes. But she hasn't been homeschooled in like three years, man. And so what?"

"Oh, naw. It's cool, it's cool," he said with his hands up. "Laurel Bennett, huh. I just never would've pictured. But hey, man, I dig it."

****

I showered after a hard day's practice. School was literally in a few days. We had this weekend left, and there was this feeling in the back of my head, this distant worry that I knew my childhood was coming to an end. I had plans of taking up with the family business— Anderson Construction and Contracting LLC—although my parents always offered college as a choice. I felt this dread and obligation all at the same time. The dread of things changing, and the obligation I felt as the only son who wasn't leaving them to struggle with my father's dream.

I tried shaking that out of my head. I wanted to enjoy the weekend with Laurel. Heck, I wanted to enjoy the year I had left because I didn't know what was on the other side of that. She had piano lessons she was giving out today with the kids, and I was going to meet her at the college. We really didn't have plans, only to meet up and see where things led from there.

"Are you going to be home for dinner?" Mom asked as I grabbed my keys off the counter.

"I think we will get something while we are out."

"Oh, you should take her to Mama Mia's, the new Italian place on Main Street," Mom said, eyes lighting up. I hadn't asked her yet about how she and Laurel knew each other, but there was something there, some kind of familiarity between them—but neither mentioned it.

"Thanks for the suggestion," I said, going through the door, realizing that was probably the exact place I smelled the delicious food from when I first heard her play and sing.

Ten minutes down the road and I picked her up at the college where she was giving lessons. I could see the last of her students being picked up by their parents. She turned toward my truck, and a smile lit up her face. There wasn't anything awkward about her, or us. I mean, I didn't really know a ton about dating, but there were plenty of cringe-worthy performances from my friends.

"Hey!" Laurel said, throwing the door on her side of the truck open and jumping up. She buckled in.

"Have you ever eaten at Mama Mia's?" I asked.

"Not yet. But it always smells so good when I walk by."

"Wanna go?" I smiled.

She tucked a loose strand of blonde hair behind her ear. "Sounds good to me."

Surprisingly, I found a spot to park on Main Street. As we walked in, the vibe of the entire place was pretty cool—old Scorsese movie posters lined the exposed brick walls, individual stained-glass lamps hung from the ceiling over each booth, and delicious smells of Italian cooking permeated the air.

"Grab a booth wherever you like," a waitress yelled at us from behind the counter while she was in the middle of grabbing stuff for one of her tables.

Spotting a booth in the corner, I suggested we go for that one.

After climbing into the booth, we both picked up a menu.

"You paying?" she asked.

"Of course," I said, smiling back at her coyness.

"Great. I'll take one of everything."

"How about one pizza?"

"Only if it has pineapple."

"Okay, okay. I see your game."

"Hey! Pineapple is the most underrated pizza topping there is."

I arched a skeptical eyebrow at her. "Mmhmm."

By this time, our waitress came over.

"What can I get you two to drink?" she asked, pad and pen in hand.

"Umm, I'll have ice water with lemon," Laurel said.

"Yeah, me too."

"Do you two know what you want, or do you need a little more time?" she asked, gazing down at her pad while she was writing.

"Yeah," I said. "I think we've settled on a large pizza with cheese, one side with pineapple and the other side with pepperoni." I gazed over to Laurel to see her smile in approval.

"All righty! I'll get your drinks right out. Give us about twenty minutes for your pie to be done. Let me know if you need anything else in the meantime."

"Well played, mister."

"I think that's a pretty good compromise," I added.

"So, you know all about me—my great love for the McKenzies, the world's cutest couple and teachers, my musical passion, and that I know without a doubt pineapple is the great underdog of pizza toppings, but I really don't know much about you. I know you play football, drive a pretty badass truck, and have extremely warm hands."

I laughed. "Warm hands? What?"

"Yeah. Your hands are warm. That's a good thing. It means the rest of you is warm too, which is also a good sign," she said, bringing the straw up to her lips.

I watched her lips form an 'o' to take a sip from her lemon water, her big eyes like saucers gazing at me, awaiting some kind of answer.

It was odd being cornered into thinking about things you never really took the time to consider before. I mean, sure, of course I liked things. I guess I was just so nondescript. And what did that say about me?

"Ugh, I dunno. Maybe ask me questions and I'll try to answer." Right at that moment, our waitress came out with a piping hot pie.

"Careful. This is hot," she said, bending over a bit, sliding it off her large oven mitt and onto the table.

The amazing aroma hit me, and my stomach growled.

"Does everything look right?"

I glanced at the pizza, up to Laurel, and then over to the waitress. "Uh, yeah, I believe so."

"Sounds good. Flag me down if you need anything. I'll be over to check on you in a few."

"Thank you," Laurel said. "You have to at least try a bite of pineapple pizza before you can legally hate on it."

I smiled. That could sum me up, my experience with Laurel. Trying things I never had before. Thinking things I never had before. *Wanting* things I never had before. "Fair enough."

She cut off a piece and guided it onto my plate. "What's your favorite movie?"

I had a few I really liked, but the one I loved and watched every year since I could remember was this Bruce Willis film my parents went on and on about going to the drive-in to see when it first came out. Since then, it had become a tradition to watch it every year. "Armageddon."

"Oh, I know that one. That's the one with the Aerosmith soundtrack, right?"

I chuckled. "Yeah, I can see why you'd remember it that way."

"Well, heck yeah. Steven Tyler? I mean, come on. Love me some Aerosmith. So, favorite food?"

I held up the pizza. "This, of course."

She bit into hers. After taking a few bites, she launched into a further investigation of things I liked. "If you could go anywhere, anywhere at all, where would you go?"

I paused for a moment, trying to digest the enormity of choices. "Like in the states or the world?"

"The world."

In this moment, I was going exactly where I wanted. I couldn't imagine any place in the world being more exciting than in this pizza joint sitting across from Laurel. "I've always thought New Zealand seemed interesting."

"The Lord of the Rings trilogy was filmed there. Oh, so wasn't The Piano, one of mine and my mom's personal favorites, for obvious reasons."

There was this part of me, this part that was curious about her mom. What happened to her? What was Laurel's whole story? There was also this warning hammering and clawing at the back of my brain telling me I was better off leaving well enough alone. Time took care of most things, so my mom always said, slow and easy wins the race. I'd find things out in time as I needed to.

"Okay, okay," Laurel said, talking between mouthfuls of pizza. "Where do you want to go for college?"

I remained silent for a moment, not sure how to really address that. "Oh, ugh, I'm not sure."

I think she could sense my comfort level dipping below where it should be. She reached over real quick and gave my hand a squeeze.

In return, I stabbed the bite of pineapple pizza on my plate with the fork and brought it to my lips where it hovered for a moment.

"Go on, chicken," she said, egging me on.

I bit down and chewed on it for a while and was surprised to find that it wasn't that bad after all.

"I think now it's my turn." I swallowed down the sample pineapple pizza bite.

"Fire away," she said, tearing into her pizza with full confidence and quite unafraid of me.

"Where would you go if you could? Anywhere in the world?"

"Boston."

"Boston?" That seemed odd. The ability to go anywhere in the world, and she still limited her choice to a place within her country.

"Sure," she said, taking a sip of her water.

"Why Boston?"

"Berklee."

"Is that like a town in Boston?"

She smiled at this. "No. Berklee is a college, a college of music, music, and more music." She seemed to drift off in a dreamy state for a brief moment before snapping back to. "But it costs like a million dollars and the acceptance rate is horrific, something like less than forty percent of applicants actually get in."

I listened to her go on and on, eyes wide and animated about dreaming of what Berklee would be like—something that she clearly wanted but knew the likelihood of going was low—and in that moment, I wished I could give her what she wanted. But there was this remote selfish beast in me I was fighting to keep suppressed. Should I name it jealousy? I didn't know what it was, but I shrugged it off, trying not to feel too guilty that Laurel's lack of financial means meant that she would stay here.

Some things in life were like that pineapple pizza—a pleasant surprise. And then some things were on the opposite end of that spectrum—scary, terrifying, and intense. And looking back, I knew what my problem was. I just didn't know how to handle it. And it cost me everything.

SASHA HIBBS

Chapter Ten

The McKenzie Experience

Brayden

I almost had time to process Laurel's squeals of delight at having the McKenzies for English—a class we lucked into having together—before Mrs. McKenzie's true to fashion, flaming hot pink lipstick smacked me in the face.

She literally was as Laurel described her. A woman who had dyed her hair so many times it had a blue hue over top the silver, bushy eyebrows I suspected she did nothing to on purpose, and the signature hot pink lipstick Laurel went on about. She was wearing what looked to be the itchiest wool skirt I'd ever seen with a matching jacket, and a pink flamingo brooch—a piece of jewelry I found out promptly was a jeweled pin women or men pinned to their shirts or coats.

Mr. McKenzie wasn't as loud in his appearance as Mrs. McKenzie. He was tall, and thin, white hair swept to the side and combed back in what looked to be the same haircut he'd likely had his entire life. He had black thick framed glasses and wore a checkered suit that screamed of suits I saw in pictures of my grandfathers from the seventies.

I didn't think I'd ever had a class where two teachers taught together.

"You are in for a treat!" Laurel said beside me with all the bubbling enthusiasm of a fangirl. She was cute.

"Hear ye! Hear ye!" Mr. McKenzie shouted theatrically with a clenched fist in the air. "All devices shall henceforth be banned in thy domain as decreed by Mrs. McKenzie!"

"Dunt duh da dunt!" Mrs. McKenzie drummed the top of her desk with heavily jeweled fingers, which made the noise all that much louder. "If ye do not abide by the law set henceforth, ye shall be sent to the barracks or worse!"

"We will be watching the one and only Man of La Mancha this semester!" Mr. McKenzie announced with over-the-top enthusiasm. I wasn't sure if this was English lit or drama.

I looked over to Laurel to gauge her reaction and was met with a big smile from her. "I guess this must be pretty good?" I asked. I'd never heard of it, or having a class with a wife-husband duo, or eating pineapple on pizza. But yet, here I sat beside my girlfriend having tried and survived the pineapple pizza, watching nervously as the McKenzies literally rolled out what had to be an antique setup consisting of a box television and a VCR player. I was kind of in shock they still had something that old stashed here and that it actually worked.

"Without further ado," Mrs. McKenzie said while Mr. McKenzie turned the lights off, "we present to you, The Man of La Mancha!"

I felt Laurel's hand make its way into mine. I sat quietly watching what seemed like an ancient musical about prisoners, chivalry, and a woman of the night named by the hero, 'Dulcinea'. Occasionally, I would glance over to see Laurel's face fully captivated by this strange musical, and the teachers she so admired, acting out alongside in sync with the movie.

I didn't really understand the movie, or the class. Yet.

Our class period was only forty-five minutes long, so this would have to be drawn out for at least a few weeks, usually by watching ten-to-fifteen-minute clips per period. Mr. McKenzie was slow to turn the lights back on, and when he did, we all struggled for a few seconds to adjust our vision back. This would be followed by a discussion after.

"I'm not sure what you'll take away from The Man of La Mancha, but we could all stand to be a little more like Don Quixote," Mr. McKenzie said, bringing Mrs. McKenzie's hand up to his lips. "And you are my Dulcinea."

There were collective, "eews", as well as collective, "awws". This by far was the strangest class I'd ever had in my school life.

"I love Don Quixote." Laurel leaned over and whispered in my ear. I looked down at her and had to struggle to look away and back to the front of the class. Her eyes were so big, her smile curving her face in such a welcoming way. All these things made it difficult for me to concentrate with her beside me.

"Now, now," Mrs. McKenzie started and then froze mid-sentence as though she'd lost her words.

"Tomorrow we will pick back up where we left off, but also things to look forward to this year are The Great Gatsby, perhaps one of the Bronte sisters," Mr. McKenzie said, looking over at Mrs. McKenzie momentarily with a look of concern before turning his attention back to the class. "Also, I'd like for you all to think about the characters, Don Quixote and Dulcinea. What sets them apart from the others? What similarities do they have? We will be working on character dissections this semester."

I noticed Mrs. McKenzie still seemed to be kind of lost in whatever thought she had that caused her to lose focus to begin with.

Mr. McKenzie walked over to her and whispered something in her ear.

She instantly looked up at him and smiled, and it

seemed to break her free from whatever trance she was in, as though Mr. McKenzie had somehow helped her to gain back her footing.

As we stood up to leave, Laurel leaned in and whispered, "See? Aren't they adorable? They are always together. Can you imagine? It's the sweetest thing."

I could see where she was coming from and had to admit their close relationship after all these years was very impressive. But there was something, something I couldn't put my finger on, some inner struggle perhaps that was hidden from plain sight. But I could see it was a burden they shared between themselves. Did one recognize another? They reminded me a bit of my own grandparents. But *their* ending was not a happy one.

Chapter Eleven

Friday Night Lights

Laurel

My dad and I loved football, but I'd never been to a high school game. I'd watched plenty of Steelers and could easily keep up with what was going on, but there was a difference in watching a football game in the comfort of your living room as opposed to a cold night on hard bleachers with screaming parents on all sides of you. I was a little out of my element.

I wondered if Brayden felt this way at the gallery during open mic. If so, he never mentioned it. I'd asked Emily to come with me, and thank God she did, and we were at least on home turf.

"Only my love for you would induce me to subject myself to this," Emily said with her nose crinkled up under the guise of disgust, but I knew she was just giving me a hard time.

"I don't know," I said loudly, so she could hear over top of the screaming people beside us. "I think it has a small-town kind of charm to it."

Emily arched a disbelieving eyebrow at me. "I'm sure you do."

I smiled at her sauciness.

"So has Romeo asked you about homecoming yet?"

"He has."

"What? And you never said anything to me?"

"Only that you and I have to pick out dresses. Dance is in two weeks," I said, matching her smugness.

"Huh? What do you mean? Like, you told him no? *We* are going instead? I'm confused," Emily said, eyebrows scrunched up.

I laughed at her. Like I'd ever leave my bestie behind.

"Me, you, and Brayden are going."

"What? No. Nu-ugh."

"Oh, yes. Yes, you are. Are you kidding? This is our senior year, and you and I planned on going to homecoming together. What I didn't plan for was Brayden Anderson. Period. So, I told him when he asked that I'd love to go with him, but that my gurl was coming too." I loved Emily. We had had each other's backs for so many years now. I couldn't imagine my life without her. Good times and bad.

"I mean, okay. I guess that's how we're rolling," she said, and I could hear the relief in her voice which made me think deep down this was a worry she'd had, that I would ditch her for Brayden. Well, I wanted Brayden, for whatever odd reason the universe seemed to throw him in my way, and I wasn't going to pass up a clear sign. But I also wasn't going to forget about the girl I'd grown up with. We were blood sisters—this disgusting ritual we did when we were seven consisted of making cuts on each other's hands, and then holding them together, the 'blood' union making us official sisters. The age of seven came before understanding bloodborne diseases, and well, just general good hygiene practices. But we were serious. And that was a commitment I was not willing to break.

"Hey! I think the home team is scoring a touchdown!" Emily screamed and I looked in the same direction in time to see the scoreboard change. I have to admit there was a small thrill of excitement coursing through me knowing Brayden was down there and happy to be winning a game that was so important to him. I searched the crowd below for his number.

Fourteen.

I could see him being pummeled by teammates in celebration of their recent score. There were a million things to be distracted by—cheerleaders, teammates, bright lights, the roaring crowd—and yet somehow his eyes searched out the crowd for me. A big smile spread across his face once our gazes locked. There was a song in there somewhere. I just knew it.

****

English with the McKenzies was my favorite. Most of the time they were substitutes floating from class to class, but for some reason this year, they were teaching senior English. Together. I really didn't care why. I was just thrilled they were.

Today Mr. McKenzie came strolling out in front of the classroom wearing a bright red cardigan with a fake mustache and a very real black hat. Hands thrown up in the air with gusto, he said, "Why should we all be a little more like Don Quixote?"

He searched the crowd, looking for an active participant. I wasn't sure what made him decide to answer his own question, but he suddenly went over to Mrs. McKenzie, grabbed her hand and faced her. "Because he is essentially good and kind regardless of those around him. He only sees this in others as well."

My heart just swelled with admiration for my favorite couple.

Mrs. McKenzie smiled up at him. "It is our great human flaw to see the bad in others over the good. But with Don Quixote, the good always triumphs in spite of so many evils. He believes so strongly, this deep-rooted belief seems to infect others in the best possible way."

The bell rang, dissipating the spell that at least I and the McKenzies seemed to be under.

"Next week! Be prepared!"

Brayden and I fell into a routine, thankfully without much awkwardness and surprisingly not too much ribbing from his friends. I rode the bus into school, we had one class together—my favorite—ate lunch together, went our separate ways. Then I would meet up with him at the end of the day. I'd never felt giddy before, but I'd be lying if I said my heart didn't flutter a bit when I walked outside to see him leaning up against his truck waiting for me, and my heart did something else entirely when he smiled at seeing me.

I was … happy. And despite losing our homecoming game to the Minutemen of Lewis County— the rival team—I believed Brayden was happy too. We were an odd pair, by most accounts, but I remembered the hand, and his warmth, and sincerity—something as a musician you strive to portray in your music, and Brayden was simply that. A living embodiment of that just walking around.

****

Emily's pap dropped her off at the house so we could get ready for the dance.

The last six weeks had been a whirlwind. Summer blended into fall. I'd never considered having a boyfriend let alone getting to go to homecoming with one.

"You look pretty badass," Emily said as we both looked at my reflection in the mirror, Zelda laying on top of my bed, gazing at both of us.

I had to admit, the dress made me feel pretty. Emily and I went to this little boutique out in the middle of nowhere, and we both picked two very different dresses. Mine—a strapless long red dress with matching converse, and Emily a long black and white satin dress with rhinestones embroidered into the hem.

"Well, you look pretty too! What do you think, Zelda?" We both turned to look at her. "Well, girl?" I leaned over and scratched between her ears.

I heard Brayden pull up. Emily and I walked out into the living room.

My dad's face softened as he walked over to me. He hugged me and then held me at arm's length. "What a vision you are. Your mother would've thought you were stunning."

I could feel the lump in my throat, and I think my father sensed it, so he momentarily pulled me in closer for another hug before releasing me.

"Emily, you clean up pretty nice too," Dad said with a lopsided smile.

"Thank you, Uncle Scott."

Brayden knocked on the door and was promptly greeted by my dad. "Hello, Mr. Bennett."

"Scott, please," Dad politely corrected him.

"Scott," Brayden repeated sheepishly.

"Listen, you better have these girls back by eleven."

"Absolutely," Brayden said, and I rushed them all out of the door before this got any more awkward.

"Love you, Dad!" I said over my shoulder.

"Have a great time." He waved as Emily and I attempted to get up into Brayden's truck as gracefully as one could in a dress.

"I didn't think to make a reservation which my mom tells me was something I was supposed to do. Do you want to try one of the places on Main Street, or do you have any suggestions?" Brayden asked.

"Actually, yes. I do," I said. "I'd like a hot fudge sundae from The Dairy Duchess." They were only open seasonally and would be closing for the year soon. It somehow seemed fitting we would go there. After all, The Dairy Duchess was where I was bold enough to ask Brayden why he'd low key stalked me for two days. Dear

God, did I have Stockholm Syndrome? I laughed to myself.

"Ice cream?" Emily asked, raising a brow.

"Mm-hmm."

"Sundaes sound wonderful."

Brayden parked and helped us down from the truck. We passed a few kids dressed up walking up and down Main Street, likely taking advantage of photo ops and going to dinner.

There wasn't a huge line. After getting our ice cream, Emily, Brayden, and I sat down at one of their outside concrete tables. Emily and I were especially careful not to let any drip on us.

"So, Brayden," Emily began. "You got any hot friends?"

Brayden choked a little bit.

I sighed inwardly. I knew my luck with Emily was going to run out at some point.

"I mean, you go to the same school as me."

"Well, that *is* true. However, I feel like you'd have more of an inside scoop. You know what I mean?"

"Emily, I don't think Brayden is exactly a matchmaker," I said through slightly clenched teeth. She'd let me off the hook for a while now, which was not in her nature. She totally was opportunistic, taking every chance she could to rib me. In all fairness, I'd have done the same to her. That's how we rolled.

"Yeah right. I don't believe that, not after Brayden hung around the gallery to hear you and then came back, and what was it you said about him hearting all your posts?"

"Emily, I swear I'm going to kill you," I said, cheeks flaming red. I flicked my gaze to Brayden, who simply seemed amused by the two of us. I was thankful he didn't appear as embarrassed as I felt. "On second thought, do you have a friend you could hook Emily up with? Like someone special? I happen to know she's a sucker for Dungeons and Dragons and likes to dress up and go to cosplay conventions."

"Really?" Brayden said, looking amused while eating his sundae.

"True story," I said, hands up to emphasize my honesty as I gladly threw Emily under the bus.

"You're just jealous because you can't rock Napoleon Dynamite as good as I can and always get stuck being Kip."

"Wait. What?" Brayden grinned as though he'd been let in on the biggest secret. Unfortunately, I was the punch line.

"Emily, you little betrayer!"

"I've got pics to prove it," Emily said. "Bwahahaha!"

"Don't you dare, Emily! I swear I'll get you back for this," I said, watching Brayden stand up to go and lean over Emily so he could see for himself what his girlfriend looked like dressed up like Napoleon Dynamite's older brother.

"Oh man, the glasses really tie the outfit together," Brayden said, glancing over at me, smiling.

"Well, ha-ha. All right. Enough having fun at my expense."

"I guess," Emily said while sporting an evil grin.

"Ready to go?" Brayden held out his hand and I didn't hesitate to place mine in his.

That warmth. It made my insides hum, much like an instrument's soul connecting with the one playing it.

Not that I'd ever been, but according to those who cared, prom was always held off campus, somewhere with a bit more polish and decor than our high school gym, but homecoming was always held here. It was a coin toss between the gym and the cafeteria. I'd come my freshman year with Emily because after being homeschooled you better believe attending homecoming was the highlight of getting to go to public school.

Sadly, it didn't live up to the fantasy I had built up in my head. After consuming a combination of Disney movies and social media, I believed homecoming was akin to being whisked off into a magical night by someone who'd waited all night for you, knowing somehow you were meant to be together like where Ariel and Prince Eric have their *kiss-the-girl* moment. Turned out there was no prince charming, I spilled this sugary punch-like drink on my rented homecoming dress ruining it, and Emily and I watched most of the kids lose their minds in what appeared to be a disgusting grind line.

Expectations versus reality. Sigh.

But tonight, tonight was different. I had my prince charming. I had my gorgeous red dress. I had cheesy dance music, disco balls and lights, and various perfumes permeating the air.

Chapter Twelve

Just Kiss the Girl

Brayden

I refused to allow bringing Emily with us to homecoming to be weird. Or better yet, maybe I was just getting good at adapting to weird situations. And, honestly, that felt okay to me. I was going with Laurel, so what did I care if her cousin and best friend, Emily, came with us? I certainly didn't have eyes or feelings for Emily. And when I picked them up at Laurel's house, all I could see was Laurel in her red dress, her face framed by her golden hair, her nervous smile that I felt was nervous because of me.

As we walked into the high school, I didn't get too much ribbing from my teammates. I think after the initial shock wore off from the fact I finally had a girlfriend, I think they were just relieved me dating was an actual possibility. Really if there was anything funny or shocking that happened, it wasn't me and Laurel finding our way to each other, but this strange electric connection made almost immediately between Chase and Emily the minute we walked through the door.

"Chase?" I heard Emily say to herself, like even she had no control over her feet or the direction they were taking her in. It seemed like she might be seeing him for the first time, or maybe it was the first time they were seeing each other.

"Do they have any classes together or …?" I trailed off, trying to mentally connect the dots.

"I don't think so," Laurel said in a small state of shock as she and I both watched this scene unfold before us.

Chase and Emily owned the dance floor. They

danced like they'd practiced in secret for all four years of high school to now finally have their magical moment. I didn't know what the hell was happening. It was like they locked eyes and some kind of voodoo magic picked up where their feet left off.

I knew Chase could shake his ass on the football field, but I'd never seen him dance the entire time we grew up. And now suddenly, while never breaking eye contact, they stomped, kicked, twirled, and spun like they'd been going to line-dancing classes in secret together all these years and tonight was their big reveal.

Laurel and I just kind of stood together in shock and awe looking at two people we were very close to, and yet they seemed to us complete strangers now.

Eventually, the dance music stopped and a slower tune took its place.

"Hmmm," I said. My hand found its way to Laurel's. I laced our fingers up. I was a bit nervous being so close to her and suddenly became aware of the intimacy dancing involved. If I could just keep my legs from shaking. "Dance?" It was all I could muster.

She answered with a smile.

We led each other on the dance floor and tried our best to move to the noise blaring out from the DJ likely doing his best too.

I had a better idea.

"Come with me," I said, as I watched her eyebrows form an arch of doubt and suspicion. "Seriously, trust me. And Emily is clearly engaged." We both looked over in their direction and while this weird connection had been going on now for a solid forty-five minutes, it was still a bit weird to acclimate to. But stranger things have happened.

I held onto her hand as we slipped through the mirror ball lit dance floor, and past other students dressed from head to toe in sequins and flashy suits, and chaperons hovering near the punch bowl watching it like a hawk, no doubt so no one would spike it, and then on into the hallway we went.

"Where in the heck are you taking me?"

I gave her a sideways smile.

"The music room?" she questioned.

"Would you mind playing a few songs for me?" I asked as we snuck into the room, keeping the lights off so we wouldn't blow our cover. There were enough outside artificial lights streaming in through the windows so we could see.

I don't know where I worked up the nerve to ask her, but since picking her up, all I could think of was listening to and watching her play the piano. She was such a natural. Laurel knew how to weave magic with music. She was an enchantress.

I could see her face soften even in the shadows and then lift in a smile. "Of course."

We both walked over to a black piano tucked away in the corner.

"Well, not quite how I envisioned homecoming," she said, pulling out the bench and lowering herself down.

"I'm sorry. We can go back to the dance." I jammed a thumb in the air behind me toward the door. I started to feel bad until she gave me a sideways glance and a coy smile. And then I breathed a sigh of relief.

"This is actually much better." She smiled and turned her attention back to the piano in front of her. "The crowd can be a little overstimulating."

I stood to the side of her, but far away enough that I hoped she didn't feel pressured or like I was lumbering over her.

"I've been working on a new piece for a few

weeks. I suppose now is as good a time as any to try it out."

I watched her slender fingers elegantly glide across the piano keys, producing a slow, harmonic sound, but when she began to sing, I was transfixed, I was transported, I was trapped. I had never been here before, but I knew as sure as I loved my parents, as sure as I never wanted to disappoint my team or coach, that Laurel was something, somewhere, *someone* I knew in my very bones. I felt it. I felt *her*. Each note she played was like a footstep toward a journey I'd been walking toward my entire life. Each word she sang only seemed to solidify that belief even more.

Somewhere within the fog, haze, and spell she was weaving, I thought to pull out my phone and record her. She'd ensnared me, but I wanted to make sure I could relive this moment. She was so wrapped up in her music that she didn't notice what I was doing.

There was a magic at play here that I'd never felt in my life. I thought back to several weeks ago when her siren song lured me from two blocks away down Main Street where she sat perched on a flower planter singing her heart out without a care in the world. That spell had only grown stronger. I wasn't afraid to call it for what it was, what I knew had been happening to me at a rapidly moving pace, but I was hesitant to share my feelings and scare Laurel off. I knew better.

Instead, I watched as the shadows danced across her soft face, the shape of her lips as they moved to expel her song, the elegant movement of her wrists and fingers—all these things captivated me, made my nerves ebb and flow like a midnight sea she was gently sailing over.

I might keep how I felt to myself for now, but I had other urges I couldn't suppress one moment longer. I shoved my phone in my pocket as her song came to an end, her head slightly bowed as she somberly looked down at the keys her fingers rested on. Her blonde hair was draped over her shoulder in such a way, she couldn't have looked any more beautiful than she did at this very moment.

Not wanting to startle her, I gently sat next to her. As she looked up, I carefully cupped her face in the palm of my hands, giving her every opportunity to break free or to accept me.

She looked at me, eyes relaxed, lips parted.

I searched her eyes, read her expression, felt her warmth in the palms of my hands.

As my heart nearly pummeled away in my chest making its own music, I lowered my head, resting my forehead against hers.

I kissed her.

SASHA HIBBS

Chapter Thirteen

Mama Always Said

Laurel

"Well, Mama, I had my first kiss," I said, sitting crossed legged on our floor of moss and ferns, scratching Zelda between the ears as she lay next to me. She always made this pilgrimage with me. And I was thankful because I knew Zelda sensed not only the pain from it, but that it was still necessary for me to communicate with my mama.

"Emily is doing good. We went to homecoming together. I wish you could've seen our dresses. Oh, and she went to band camp. Her pap is still cranky, but good. Mama, I'm a senior this year. Can you believe it? Soon, I'll be going to college, at least I hope to. Do you remember us always talking about Berklee? Well, it's crazy expensive and no way in this world could we ever afford it, but they offer scholarships. I mean, they are competitive, but I'm going to try. Right? Isn't that what you'd tell me to do? And Dad, well, he's Dad. He's still crazy making art, and he's completely lost without you." Tears burned in my eyes. My parents love story was one for the ages.

It was my favorite fairytale of all time—the love story of my parents. It was everything ordinary and epic all at once, the cosmos shot two stars that collided, collided and ended up being my parents.

One day my dad walked into the McDonald's she was working at, but the universe was at play because my dad always drove through the drive thru. He never walked in. But he said he saw the prettiest blonde he'd ever seen through the window, and time stopped. He said it was as if the world slowed down to a complete halt, and as he walked through the doors, she slowly turned toward him. A Led Zeppelin song was echoing off in the distance somewhere, belting out what would become the anthem of their life together. And he knew the minute their eyes locked, starbursts and sunbeams and all the magic in the world hummed around the two of them, binding them together forever. Soulmates lost in a previous life finally reunited in this one. Or at least they found each other in a McDonalds at Nutter Fort, West Virginia.

Mama talked his head off, and that night when he went home, he told his best friend he'd met the girl he was going to marry, and while attending a Steve Miller Band concert in Pittsburgh, they both decided they couldn't live in the universe together without each other.

Cosmic love. That's what Mama always said.

It was only Zelda, myself, and Mama's headstone, so I let the tears slip from my eyes. My heart ached. My mother was so beautiful. Her soul shined brightly, and I swear that light somehow shone from her like her whole body was surrounded by a halo. She loved me something fierce, and there were days when I forgot she was no longer with us and the remembering part took my breath away. It hurt so bad.

"Mama, his name is Brayden," I said through quivering lips. "Brayden Anderson."

Mama always said the universe liked a good foreshadowing, so it would certainly make sense then that I knew his mother before knowing him. She was the Easter egg, I guess. I thought back to the day, the worst day of my life, when I met Brayden's mom. Never in a million years did I think she'd enter it again.

I stood up and picked the weeds around her tombstone. She loved nature, loved how green and lush our mountain was, and so it only made sense that Dad buried her here.

There were so many things she used to say to me, so many times I would let what she had to say go in one ear and out the other. I never thought there would come a day when she wasn't here to nag at me, to scold me, to love me.

Zelda stood up and leaned against me. I knew she was trying to comfort me.

"You know what Mama always said, Zelda?" I scratched her between her ears.

She looked up at me with those big, brown, knowing eyes.

"She always said you'd never miss the water until the well ran dry."

Rubbing my hand across her cold headstone, all I could think of was there were never truer words.

SASHA HIBBS

Chapter Fourteen

An Eternal Love

Brayden

These past few months with Laurel were the happiest of my life. Being with her even somehow made our losing football season something I never really dwelled on. I mean, sure, it would've been cool to win, especially my senior year when it mattered most, but somehow, I felt like I had already won the lottery.

It was Christmas and I was struggling with what to get her.

"Mom, I need help," I said, shoving my hands through my hair.

She glanced up from the magazine she was reading. "Yeah? What with?"

"I don't know what to get Laurel for Christmas, and I just don't want to get her something lame like jewelry or flowers, or I don't know." Laurel was so different. She was too cool for pricey expensive things, not that she didn't deserve them and not that I didn't wish I could shower her with whatever she wanted, but material things didn't impress her. And I was drawn to her for that.

Mom smiled up at me. "Well, if it's coming from you, I'm sure she won't think it's lame."

"You know what I mean." I actually whined. "Please." I put my hands together, begging.

"Well, you know she loves music and instruments, and she loves art. What are some other things she likes?"

"She likes antiques."

"Okay, okay. I think we can work with this." Mom got up from her chair and laid the magazine down.

"Let's go."

"Now?"

"You got something better to do?"

"No."

"Then chop, chop, mister." Mom snapped her fingers at me.

Twenty minutes later, Mom pulled into the antique mall in Hodgesville, a huge building I remember being at once.

It had been a pretty mild winter so far. We walked into the antique mall and the smell was the first thing that hit me. It wasn't a bad smell, just a very specific one, one of old wood and memories stored in one huge warehouse. I walked through booth after booth, pausing momentarily, looking at old photos. I never could understand how they ended up in an antique store for sale. I mean, these were people's families.

I heard familiar voices in the next booth over. I glanced up and watched my mom inspecting a doily. I moved closer out of the current booth I was looking at and over to the one where I heard the McKenzies at.

"Oh, Jimmy will love this!" Mrs. McKenzie said, clutching onto a small, shiny silver object I couldn't make out.

Mr. McKenzie gave her a sad smile but said nothing.

They didn't notice me. I watched them leave that booth and move on to another.

I walked in and looked around. My gaze landed on a painting that held me captive. It was of a couple, sitting down, but in a way that the woman was leaning into the man, like a lover's embrace. They had the appearance of a couple from maybe the nineteen twenties. It was framed in an old metal frame where a heavy coat of green paint was peeling at the corners, revealing a pretty patina.

Mom came around the corner. "Oh, that *is* pretty!"

"This is the one I want for her," I said, looking over my shoulder at Mom and then back to the Christmas present I was going to buy for Laurel. I knew she would love it. She talked all the time about how art 'speaks' to you and when it does, you have an obligation to listen. I'd never considered art, or much music really, until meeting Laurel. I'd never had pineapple pizza. I'd never had Laurel in my life, and now that she was in it, I couldn't imagine a place with her out of it.

"I'll go grab someone from the counter to get it down," Mom said.

"I don't mind getting someone, or maybe I can reach it—"

"No, it's fine," she said.

I didn't stop her. I suspected she wanted to take a look at that doily again as it was closer to the counter. I'd have to get that for her for Christmas.

I was gazing at the painting I was going to purchase for Laurel when Mom and the attendant came around the corner.

"He died during Desert Storm," the man said. "He loved collecting coins, and they come in here once a month to buy him a new coin."

"How terribly sad," Mom said.

"She's been like this for the last six months and each time I see her, she seems to be getting worse."

Mom just shook her head. Were they talking about the McKenzies?

"That's the one." Mom pointed to the painting.

"Ah, *Love Eternal*. Nice one," he said, setting up his step ladder and retrieving the painting.

"I think she'll love it," Mom said.

"I hope so."

After paying, I asked Mom to go on ahead of me. I grabbed her doily, this thin lace napkin looking thing, and paid at the counter. "Have a nice day," I said, walking out with Christmas purchased for both ladies in my life.

I popped the trunk and carefully laid my gifts in a way they shouldn't get too rattled around. I slid into my seat and buckled up.

"Sure you don't want me to drive?"

"Someday when I can't anymore, like Mrs. McKenzie, you can drive me all over the place, but for now, I can drive just fine."

"Mrs. McKenzie?"

"She was in there buying coins for her son that died years ago."

"What do you mean?"

"I mean she doesn't remember that he's dead. He died while on active duty during Desert Storm. She has early onset dementia."

I sat back and watched out the window as Mom drove down Rt. 20 just kind of letting that information sink in, knowing what it meant. I didn't know a whole lot about diseases in general, but that one hit close to home. With grandparents on both sides that suffered from and ultimately succumbed to dementia, I was somewhat familiar with what that looked like. I was very young, but I remembered my grandparents. I remembered they were fine and then suddenly they weren't. But time was also a warped reality to a child.

I thought back to the beginning of class, and my time with them as teachers. While thinking about it, it was Mr. McKenzie who did most of the teaching. I remembered her having moments where she just seemed lost, and he would whisper something into her ear, maybe some kind of reassurance that would pull her out of whatever part of her mind she was currently trapped in.

Dammit.

This was going to hurt Laurel. She loved the McKenzies. Mr. McKenzie … dammit. To have lost your only kid, and now to watch the slow and steady decline of your wife who never remembered the tragedy they shared… I was in no hurry to tell Laurel. I suddenly found myself wanting to be in Don Quixote's world where chivalry and good deeds existed, where nothing but the best outcome prevailed, where dementia wasn't the end.

I thought about the painting of the two embracing lovers and imagined it to have been the McKenzies in another life.

An eternal love.

SASHA HIBBS

Chapter Fifteen

Christmas Morning

Laurel

"No, no. I am fine!" Dad said while brushing me off. "I've absolutely enjoyed my morning with my girl. You come back this evening and we will have dinner together," Dad said, holding onto the flannel pajama bottoms and Whitman's Sampler I got him for Christmas. "I sure hope you liked your gift."

"Are you freaking kidding me?" I said, running my hands up and down the beautiful sunburst finish on my vintage Martin guitar. I knew we didn't have a ton of money, and it had to cost him more than what he could afford. But Dad was prideful in that way and would be insulted if I made a fuss over money and him buying me gifts. It was beautiful. "I love it!"

I pulled the guitar up and sat it gently across my lap, allowing my fingers, who knew the soul of an instrument by touch, to caress the neck, and then I poised my hands to play it. I let my fingers glide up and down while I sang Dad's favorite Christmas song, *Home for the Holidays*.

"Beautiful," he said, a smile underneath his beard that was as broad as it was wide. I loved my dad, and me loving him sure made me miss my mom even more. She should've been here with us, celebrating, laughing, telling me that she loved whatever silly gift I got her. I didn't have a lot of experience losing someone and nor did I want it, but I felt confident that the holidays were the worst for longing and missing the ones you loved most.

"Thank you." I laid my guitar back down in its case.

"Well, you get out of here so you can get back,"

Dad said as there was a light rapping on the door. "Me and Zelda are going to be here taking it easy."

I opened the door to see Brayden on the other side of it, smiling the moment our eyes met. "Merry Christmas," he said, a small gift in his hands.

"Come in." I stepped out of the way so he could move past me.

"Merry Christmas," Brayden said to my dad. "This is from my family." He handed over the small gift.

Dad accepted it and sat it down beside him. "Mom also says you are welcome to come over for dinner. We'd love to have you." I was so happy Brayden was less awkward around Dad. It took some time, but things finally progressed to a natural state.

"Please tell your mom I said thank you. It's much appreciated. But I have to visit with my wife."

My heart ached at the thought of my dad making this pilgrimage alone. It was always a hard one.

Brayden never commented, and really, what could you say?

"Daddy—"

He cut me off. "We will be here when you get back. You go have fun," he said, and I knew he was referring to my mama's grave being here, for the woman we both loved was long gone.

I ran over quickly and hugged him. I whispered into his ear, "I love you, Papa."

He hugged me back. "I love you too, girl of mine."

I had to get out of here or I was going to start crying, and I knew this entire exchange had to be weird for Brayden.

"I'll be back this evening," I said, going out the door. I don't know what Brayden thought. I never asked him. It was sometimes easier not talking, and there's no way he could relate or understand, so I simply avoided the topic. He knew my mother was dead, and that's all there was to it. If he was satisfied with that, then so was I.

"So, what's on the menu?" I asked as I strapped on my seatbelt, trying to change gears in my mind before things completely derailed.

"Well, I do love my mom's cooking. We always have ham, these roll things she makes, pumpkin pie, these cheesy potatoes you will love. I think you'll be satisfied." Brayden tilted his head and gave me a sly smile.

I gave him a sincere smile back and then gazed out the window, watching as we passed familiar house after house. I wondered what everyone else's Christmas looked like.

Since my mom died, I would look at the outside of a house and wonder what the inside looked like. What were the families like residing within? Was everyone still alive? What were their holiday traditions? Had tragedy struck them the same way it did me, as it did Dad? No. I couldn't believe anyone went through what Dad and I did, what happened, her slow decay, how she left us. No. I didn't believe it was possible. My dad and I were alone in that particular field of grief. And everything turned to a barren landscape of gray and misery should we linger in that field too long.

We rode in silence, but that was okay.

Brayden laid his warm hand on my leg, and it wasn't perverted, it was comforting. I had to give it to Brayden, aside from the occasional kiss, he never tried anything with me. There was never any pressure, just acceptance for what we were to each other, what naturally occurred between us, and I valued him so much for it.

I'd been too lost in my own thoughts to realize we

were already at his house.

I didn't wait for Brayden to come around and open my door as he was sometimes prone to do. We both got out of the truck at the same time, but he still came around, grabbed my hand, and led me into his house.

And when I walked in, this, *this* is what I felt was always on the other side of the proverbial window, the actually being involved instead of always looking in. Their house was buzzing with warmth, the smell of delicious food in the air, sights and sounds and everything Christmas. My chest constricted a bit thinking about leaving my dad to come to this. He shouldn't be all alone. He should still have a wife, and me a mother.

Dammit. Dammit. Dammit. My mom would be disappointed in my thoughts, but she was riddled all throughout them. I was angry to wake up Christmas morning and find myself in a world without her in it. I'd been robbed. And I knew I would always look at her loss that way, as though some divine thief stole what wasn't theirs.

What right did the universe have to extinguish what to me and in my heart was their brightest star? None. And I would always be bitter about that light that was taken from me.

I tried pulling myself back together. I didn't want my sorrow to make Brayden, or his family, feel uncomfortable.

"Merry Christmas!" Brayden's mom came over and gave me a squeeze. She was a total mom with her ugly Christmas sweater on and hair in a messy bun. I could tell she'd been cooking all day.

"Merry Christmas." I hugged her back.

"I was hoping your dad would come. We will send you back with a plate of food for him," she said, smiling warmly at me. Brayden was lucky, so very lucky.

Mrs. Anderson was a wonderful person with such a bubbly personality. She just always seemed ... *happy*.

"I know he will love that," I said. "He's a sucker for some homemade food."

"Well, well, let's all eat! I've got mashed potatoes for days, and ham, and these damned crescent rolls that are harder than all get out to make, and homemade pumpkin pie," she said. Then she leaned in close to whisper in my ear, "Well, as homemade as a can of pumpkin with instructions and a recipe on the back is." And then she winked like this was a secret just between the two of us. She was adorable and I appreciated how at home they always made me feel. Brayden ... he was home. I felt that when I held his hand, when I was in his presence, when he watched me perform. All those moments that added up, all those bricks that laid a foundation, all the construction that went into making a home, and when I looked to Brayden, I could see he was the builder behind it ... a home I wanted to live in someday.

"You are gonna love my mama's potatoes," he said, smiling like a little kid which in turn made me smile at his excitement.

Turned out, he was right. I ate two servings of what was the best, most cheesiest, most savory potatoes I'd ever eaten in my life. I didn't know what hit me. "Brayden, well, it's just this simple: I need the recipe."

Mrs. Anderson laughed. "It's a secret." She winked at me again.

"Well, it *is* Christmas," I said, hopeful that would sway her.

"Indeed, it is," Brayden's dad, Matt, said. "I think it's time to sit back and try to digest some of this food." He stretched while simultaneously patting his stomach. "Maybe we can go to the living room and open gifts while partially going into a food coma."

"Hell yeah," Caleb said, shoving himself away from the table and picking out the first comfy seat in the living room.

I followed the rest of them in there and sat on the floor beside Brayden. He wasn't a kid by any stretch, but I found it endearing at how he attempted to hide his enthusiasm. I'd hoped this childlike wonder in him, this happiness, never died. Mine nearly had when my mom passed away. It's funny or not, I guess, at how fast death seems to kill the remnants of childhood, forcing you to grow up quickly. Things are only enjoyable when you are with the ones you love, and what holiday made you miss your family more than Christmas?

But I didn't want to ruin this for Brayden, or his family. My pain was mine alone.

Caleb tore into his presents much like he was a little kid too.

It was fun for me to sit back and watch them, but Christmas just wasn't the same. And I guess that's what I needed to accept. I'd needed to find a way to accept that for years, I had my mom, we had each other, and we always had a wonderful Christmas. The last one, she was pretty sick, but she was still with us, and we were all together. I could see her now, watching and listening to me sing and play whatever instrument I had at the moment.

She always shed a tear—sometimes more—saying it was a bit of joy she was giving back as though throwing roses onto the stage for me performing.

"Hey, you." Brayden gently nudged my shoulder with his. "I've got something for you."

"Oh." I smiled, realizing I had been lost in my thoughts, the past always there with me, distracting me from the here and now. "Sorry."

"Don't be sorry. This is for you." Brayden handed me over a gift that I could tell he wrapped himself. His mother's gifts had neat lines and bows, but this gift showed the underside of the wrapping paper which was taboo for a gift wrapper, and it was overall just plain sloppy, like it had been wrapped by a five-year-old.

And I loved it.

His childlike sense of wonder made me despise Christmas a little less.

I gently opened the present at each corner, unsure of what it was. When I finally tore through the tape on the backside, I gently flipped it over on my lap so I could remove the rest of the paper to reveal the gift within.

I felt the smoothness of a frame, recognizing that feel with hands that never forgot before I gazed into what was in between the frame.

"It's how, it's how I feel about … you," Brayden nervously whispered in my ear.

I was staring down into the gaze of two lovers, embracing. It was the profile of a woman—I'd say nineteen-twenties, or early thirties—sitting, leaning back against her lover, one arm draped down relaxed, and the other upright, his hand cupping hers. He was leaning in, whispering sweet nothings into her ear, giving her gentle kisses along the neck like a lover would. You could tell the artist intended to let the viewer know the male subject was smitten, and the object of his affection was the beautiful girl with pinned up curls lovingly resting up against him.

I was touched. I was, but I was something else, something more.

Breaking the spell, his mom said, "Would you mind playing a little something for us?"

I looked up in a bit of a daze. "Oh, ugh, I'm so sorry, I didn't bring anything with—"

"It's used, but Matt and I got you a little something. Maybe you can keep it here and play every now and then."

Matt pulled out a used ukulele with a little red bow situated around the neck. "Merry Christmas from all of us."

I accepted the small guitar, the feel of the wood never old against my skin. I always made up stories in my mind to go along with the feeling I had when I made contact with someone else's instrument, like they had souls, vibrant souls that were telling me stories.

"Oh wow," I said, looking down at the K emblem branded on the head of the ukulele. I didn't know what Matt meant by used, or God in heaven, what he paid for it, but a Kanile'a ukulele was top of the line as far as sound and quality went. "What a beautiful instrument." I tuned it up, feeling the elegance and smoothness brush against me as I did so.

"Will you take a request?" Caleb asked.

"Sure."

"I always loved Silver Bells. Can you play that?" Caleb asked.

"Can she play that?" Brayden said, blowing a raspberry—something I'm sure to this point in our relationship, I'd never seen him do. "She can play anything you ask her to."

There was this level of confidence in my playing ability from him that made me feel in ways I never had. Did I know what love in that way was? I didn't know. I didn't want to give those feelings a name. So, instead, I raised the ukulele to my chest and began strumming the familiar Christmas tune.

I sang about silver bells and Christmas day, city lights and music all the while staring into the portrait of what was a nineteen thirties version of what I pictured

THE TRUTH ABOUT FIREFLIES

Brayden and I to be.
      Two lovers.
      Eternally.

SASHA HIBBS

Chapter Sixteen

Always His Dulcinea

Brayden

Things got weird. Somewhere between Homecoming and Christmas, Emily and Chase became a couple. A disgusting, gross, inseparable, PDA couple. I mean, I guess I was fine with it. I liked Emily, but Chase kept her busy, which meant she wasn't always the third person with me and Laurel. We all even sometimes went out together.

When I was a kid, time would drag on and on. My parents always said the older I got, the faster time would fly, to slow down and enjoy my youth. And I have to say, the older I became, the more I believed their words.

With it being February, I felt that reality was closing in on me. I hadn't built up the courage yet to talk to Laurel about what her concrete plans for the future were. I didn't want to ruin our bliss. Or what I thought at the time was a mutual bliss. I never took the time to consider she was in agony, a pain that I was gradually causing her and refusing to let up on.

"Well, now we are at the end, fair audience, what say you? Is there honor? Nobility? Courage? All these traits if you entered this classroom without, surely you will leave with them now," Mr. McKenzie said, dressed again as the part of Don Quixote. "In a world filled with unkindness, be kind. In a world void of honor, have it! In a world full of cowards, be the one with courage and watch the tides turn."

Laurel was fully captivated by this speech, and I had to admit, it was compelling, but something else had my attention—Mrs. McKenzie, who was sitting behind the desk looking a bit disheveled and confused. It had been two months since my mom made me aware of the real culprit plaguing her—dementia.

I wasn't a neurologist, not even close. I was just a teenager who at a young age lost grandparents to the disease, but if that was an indicator, I knew in my heart, Mrs. McKenzie was living on borrowed time. She'd already been six months into the school year, and if my grandparents were the measuring stick for the amount of time you had, Mrs. McKenzie had already exceeded that.

"I want a one-page report turned in by the end of this month telling me your thoughts and feelings about Don Quixote. What made him stand out? What qualities do you see in him that you see in yourself? I just want to hear how his actions made you feel. Tell me about Dulcinea. How did she influence Don Quixote? I want to know your thoughts about The Man From La Mancha in general." I watched him look over his shoulder at Mrs. McKenzie, and I don't know what he saw when he gazed at her, but he abruptly turned about and announced. "That will be all for today. I will not see you all until sometime next week."

Kids jetted up all around Laurel and I and shuffled out the door into the hallway to go who knows where—the bathroom to hide out until the next period or skip for the rest of the class. Who knew? But Laurel and I lingered for a few moments and watched Mr. McKenzie go directly to Mrs. McKenzie, who was standing up by the desk now and looking confused. You could tell Mr. McKenzie was trying to shield her from view.

I gently put my hand on Laurel's elbow to hopefully encourage her to follow me out of the room. It was clear to me Mr. McKenzie wanted privacy.

"Wait. What?" Laurel said under her breath. I could hear the confusion in her voice as we turned the corner, and I caught a glimpse of Mrs. McKenzie. Her skirt was wet from what I'm sure was an accident.

"Laurel, I'll tell you about it after we get out of here," I whispered to her.

Thankfully, she didn't fight me. After we filed out into the hallway, I walked in the direction of the library, Laurel right beside me.

"Mrs. McKenzie is sick," Laurel said, but not in a matter-of-fact way, more in like she was in disbelief and saying the words out loud, as if it was helping her piece together what she just saw.

"Yes, I think so," I said, walking beside her until we could get into the library. "Laurel, a few months ago, when I was with Mom Christmas shopping..." I sighed, shoving my hands through my hair and then scrubbing my face. "I ran into the McKenzies and I overheard her talking about her son, her son that died in war overseas. But she was talking about him like he was still alive."

"What?"

Laurel knew where I was going with this. I could see a storm brewing in her—the clouds in her eyes called confusion, hurt, and a shitty understanding of what was really taking Mrs. McKenzie down. "She has dementia, and has had it, I'd say for this entire school year which would explain why Mr. McKenizie has been allowed to teach with her instead of them teaching separately."

I could see Laurel calculating the math in her head, crunching numbers, knowing that Mrs. McKenzie was living on borrowed time. Her eyes grew red, and I could see her fighting to keep the tears at bay. This crushed her. I knew it. I felt it, felt Laurel's sorrow as if we were tied together.

"But she is his Dulcinea," Laurel said, lips quivering.

I pulled her into my chest and rested my chin on top of her head. "Of course. And no matter what happens, she will always be his Dulcinea. Dementia takes most things away, but not that, not a love between two people like the one they have." I didn't know where this speech was coming from, but as I held Laurel and tried to comfort her, I felt a warmth in my chest, and a sort of completeness. I didn't know what else to call it but … love.

****

It turns out Mr. McKenzie wasn't back in a week, not even in two weeks. The last time he addressed the class, he assigned us homework: he said he wanted a one-page report on our thoughts and feelings about Don Quixote. He wanted us to tell him what made him stand out, if we saw something of ourselves in him. How he, as a character, made us feel, and if so, what?

It had been a long time since I dressed in my three-piece black suit. I stood up. Laurel remained sitting. I thought about what Coach Westfall would say at a time like this, and I knew what my mom did say to me before picking Laurel up. She said, *"It's hard to share pain and see pain. But no matter how singular you feel the event is, you'll find out you really were never alone. Pain is universal. So is love."*

I kept replaying her words over and over in my head as I walked up to the pulpit. I avoided eye contact on my way up there only because as it turned out, it *was* hard to see other people's pain. It's such a personal thing. I inhaled deeply, pulling out a folded piece of paper. I unfolded it and smoothed out the wrinkles. I let out a long sigh as I gathered the courage to look out into what seemed a vast sea of sadness.

"Don Quixote stands out because of his unwavering and innocent belief in chivalry. He lives in a time where good deeds are not done, where people hurt each other, where doing the right thing isn't what keeps people in check, but instead cowardice is. And he, an aging man who should be disillusioned, instead takes up a coat of arms, a banner so to speak, and revives chivalry. He stands up in the face of opponents far greater than him in strength, but his intentions are good, and somehow against all possible odds, goodness prevails. He is a champion for the poor and less fortunate. Regardless of her being treated as though she has no value, he dubs an unfortunate woman a princess and names her, Dulcinea, and fights with courage, with honor, with dignity. But the reality is, we watch his mind go from reality, to fantasy, back to the bitter reality. But what I've learned is that there are some things, *virtuous things*, you find in fantasy, that you can live out in the real world. Treating people kindly. Being fair and just. Standing up for the less fortunate. These were all things that made Don Quixote, Don Quixote. Thank you, Mr. McKenzie, for showing us that Don Quixote is not a fictional character, but an idea that can live on in all of us. That we can choose to do good by each other, to be brave when it's hard. To do better. To *be* better. And for all of us to aspire to have our own Dulcinea in life to fight for."

He sat there, a man lost, amid a sea of black and of tears, of the sounds of the end of an era, and the unveiling of the next. Laurel stood up, ukulele in hand and stopped within arm's length of me. Her face was tear-stained and even in her grief, she looked beautiful.

I watched as Mr. McKenzie stood on what seemed like a shaky frame that aged significantly overnight, slowly shuffling over to the casket holding the love of his life. He bent down and kissed her forehead and remained there, staring down at all he held dear, looking at her in her eternal slumber.

As Laurel began playing and then singing the familiar tune that made the room erupt in tears, I knew in my heart of hearts, not only was Mr. McKenzie saying goodbye for now to his Dulcinea, but my own Dulcinea was standing by me, alive and well. And I admired Mr. McKenzie but witnessing his pain—I certainly didn't envy him.

As I listened to her haunting voice lift up higher and higher, I knew she would always be my Dulcinea.

I just didn't know if I'd ever live up to being her Don Quixote. And as it turned out, I didn't realize the depth of her grief, and maybe it was because I couldn't recognize my own. But I would learn. I would find out soon enough.

Chapter Seventeen

The After

Laurel

It took more energy than I realized to make it through Mrs. McKenzie's funeral. My heart burst over and over again to see Mr. McKenzie, aged and withered, become even more so, like all the youthfulness his wife seemed to help him maintain was drained out of him the moment she left. When I looked at the McKenzies, I always felt like the universe was giving me a glimpse of what my own parents would've had with each other had Dad and I not been robbed of my mother. I would look at those two and daydream about my own parents.

Imagining if only…

I was quiet riding back home in Brayden's truck, and I felt bad because I knew he didn't know what to do with my silence. But there was this damn knot in my throat, one that I knew I couldn't fight against if I attempted to speak. I looked out the window, thankful there was warm sun beaming through on my face. After days and days of gray blahness in February, these few moments where we were blessed with rays of sun were treasured.

"Laurel?" Brayden said, keeping one hand on the wheel while he slowly lowered his other on my lap, finding a loose hand so he could intertwine our fingers together.

I looked over at him, still not in enough control of my voice to answer him.

I could see he was struggling with what to say too, which made my heart ache. I kept replaying the beautiful words he read in tribute to Mrs. McKenzie, and I was so proud, so touched. I swallowed hard, trying to shove that damn knot way down where it couldn't do any damage. "I'm sorry, Brayden," I said, and my damn lips started to quiver.

"Don't be. It's hard to lose people, people you love and respect. And admire."

"It's just... It's just..." And the war was over. I started crying, a sob escaping my throat and hot tears streaming from my eyes.

Brayden pulled over into a wide spot alongside the road and put the truck in park. He kept it running thankfully for the heat. "Hey, come here," he said, taking off his seatbelt and scooching closer to me.

I took off my seatbelt too and slid over to him. When I finally reached him, I tucked my face into the crook of his neck and sobbed.

He traced little circles on the small of my back.

"I always imagined," I said through tears and a shaky voice, "that my parents would've been the McKenzies. I know it sounds stupid, but it just feels like my mom has died all over again. I used to pretend I was looking at my mom in the future had she lived, and now Mrs. McKenzie is gone and it just reminds me Mom is gone, and seeing Mr. McKenzie's pain was like my dad's, and, and, and..." I started full-on crying again.

"Hey, it's okay. It's okay," Brayden whispered into my ear, trying to sooth me.

He didn't know about my mom. There were only a few people who did. I knew people talked, spread rumors or their own version of what they thought the truth was. But in the end, it didn't matter. What did I care about the opinions of others? My mother loved me, and I loved her. And I had days where remembering the whole of it stole the breath from me, the pain of it overtaking my senses.

And I was spent.

Utterly spent.

Brayden dropped me off. He even offered to stay, but really, I just wanted to lay down with Zelda by me. She had a way of providing comfort that I believed only a dog knew how to do. It was eerie.

As I walked in the house, I sat my ukulele case down and a big white envelope with my name on it caught my attention.

Ms. Laurel Bennett

I picked up the envelope with the familiar Berklee emblem. Time was running out. For so many things. It ran out for my mom. It ran out for the McKenzies. It was running out on me. And as I lay down on my bed, exhausted, curled up to our sweet, sweet girl, I felt the smallest of knots on Zelda's stomach.

Time.

I fell asleep, rubbing my hands through her soft fur thinking time was something we all wished we had more of.

SASHA HIBBS

Chapter Eighteen

The Hard Truth

Brayden

I would've stayed with Laurel as long as she would've let me. I didn't know what to say to her, and I knew she was hurting. But in the end, after the funeral, she wanted to go home and be alone. And I got it. Really. I did. I didn't want to suffocate her, and I didn't know how to help her grieve, but as much as I understood her need to be alone, I guess it was me who didn't want to be alone. But for selfish reasons.

I shoved myself off my bed and walked into the kitchen with the sole purpose of getting some water and coming back to my room to think everything over, but Mom sat quietly at the end of the kitchen table like she'd been expecting me.

"Hi, honey," Mom said, looking up at me with knowing, sad eyes.

"Hey."

"I find in times like these, the best thing we can do is eat chocolate," she said, getting up from the table. "I saved you a piece of my German chocolate cake."

She knew that was my favorite, and had been since I could remember.

"Here," she said, sitting it down on the opposite end of the table. "I think you'll need some milk to go with that."

I sat down and watched her pour me a tall glass of milk.

"Thank you, Mom," I said, thinking about Laurel, Laurel's mom, Mrs. McKenzie, and suddenly a spasm shot through my chest at the briefest of thoughts of what it would be like to lose my own mom. I hated the thought. I was actually terrified at that moment just thinking about it. And between the cake, the milk, and the heaviness of the day, like a little boy again, I reached out and grabbed my mom, pulling her to me in a bear hug. "I love you, Mom."

"Oh, honey!" she said, wrapping warm, familiar, maternal arms around me, gently twirling a strand of my hair like she used to when I was little and she was tucking me in for bed. "I love you, too."

I felt the warmness build in the corner of my eyes, my vision getting misty, and I felt if I just clung onto my mom, she'd never be able to leave me. She'd live forever.

"It's okay, honey. It's gonna be okay."

"But how do you know?" Holding onto my mom like that little boy of yesterday, I felt small and vulnerable. I started asking her a million things at one time. How did she know everything was going to be okay? How did she know Laurel's grief would subside? How did she know mine would never be created to begin with? How did she know life just simply went on?

"Because, life doesn't just continue," she said, gently tearing away from me and holding me at arm's length. "It prevails."

"What do you mean?"

"Life is full of sadness, sorrow, and heartache, but there is a balance. You can stack all those up against one thing, and that one thing is mighty and all powerful and will always come out on top. Do you know what that is?"

"No."

"Love," she said, cupping my face and planting a kiss on my forehead. "Love will always exist in this world to balance out all the pain and sadness. It may feel buried deep down by all those other things we have to live with too, but I promise you, love always comes out fighting. Love always wins."

"Mama." I hadn't called her that in years. "I love Laurel."

"Of course you do. Your mind wouldn't be so troubled if you didn't." She smiled a knowing smile at me.

She pulled out the chair beside me and sat down. Before I knew it, over a cold glass of milk and my mother's homemade German chocolate cake, I poured my heart out to her about Laurel.

"I don't know what to do, or how to help her. I just love her so much. She adored Mrs. McKenzie. I'm also afraid of, of, of…" I swallowed hard as I tried to spit out feelings I barely understood myself. "…losing her."

"Honey," my mom said, a worried expression falling across her face. "Why are you afraid of losing Laurel?"

I shoved a piece of cake into my mouth. If I were chewing, it kept me from answering uncomfortable questions. But, eventually, I swallowed, and I had to answer. "I don't know. She's smart. She's crazy talented. What would she ever do here in this town?"

"What do you mean? Are you saying you're afraid she's not going to stay here after graduation? Or that you are, and she isn't? Or what are you saying, exactly?"

"I guess," I answered. The heavy weight of the truth I'd been carrying around was now finally out there. "Why would she stay here? What's here? And what would I do? How fair would that be for me to pressure her to stay here when I know she has these crazy skills, and the whole world should know it too, but I love her and the thought of her leaving me, forgetting me, I just can't, I don't want to think, I can't—" I felt warm tears build in the corners of my eyes, and it was accompanied by this gnawing, hollow aching in my chest.

"Brayden Anderson." My mom cupped either side of my face, turning my gaze up to hers. "Oh, honey. I believe you love her, and I can see where the agony is coming in at, but sweetheart, just because Laurel—if she does—might go off to some other college not around here to pursue her musical aspirations doesn't mean that's the end for you two."

"But she will meet other people," I said, a knot of anxiety building in my stomach. "I remember her mentioning wanting to pursue college in passing, and Caleb talking about Juilliard or whatever it was. It doesn't matter. What does Buckhannon, West Virginia have to offer someone like Laurel?"

"Of course she will meet other people. And so, what if she does? And Buckhannon has a lot to offer. It might not have a prestigious music program that produces grammy winning geniuses, but there's more to life than just that. You are putting the cart before the horse."

"But when she meets other people, she will see how ordinary I am." I said it, another truth I felt that ran to my core. Laurel was so special, so amazing, unearthly almost, and I couldn't ever measure up to that. Deep down I felt I didn't deserve her. I didn't feel like I was her equal.

"Don't ever let me hear those words come out of your mouth again," Mom said, tears forming in her eyes. "Brayden Anderson, you are a good human. You do what is right in a world full of wrong. *You* are everything that is kind and good, and I have no doubt these are all qualities someone like Laurel sees in you. So, you can't play an instrument. That doesn't define who you are as a person. What *you* have is a big heart. What *you* are is a good friend. *You* make all the difference. And there is nothing ordinary about *you*. Your ability to love is nothing short of extraordinary. Laurel can play anything she lays her hands on, but a cold instrument isn't the same as a warm heart that is genuine. Don't you ever forget that. And you have your own future to work out. I know you, and I know your heart. Would I want you to go to college? All I want is for both my kids to be happy, safe, and secure. And whether that means a future in college, or a trade, or a job, I don't know. I have full faith that you'll figure it out."

"But what about Dad?" I asked, feeling like a little boy again, looking to my mom like she held all the wisdom of ages, would know all the answers. Honestly, the thought of having to make my own life decisions was terrifying.

"What about him?" she asked, her head tilted to one side.

"I mean, for as long as I can remember, I was just always going to take up the family business."

"Sweetheart," Mom began, her voice softening, "you listen to me. If going into business with your dad is something you want, then we both want that for you. What we don't want is you tailoring your life to accommodate what you think *we* want. Your dad's business isn't going anywhere. It's yours to learn should you want, and if not, life goes on. Do you understand me? All we want is your health and happiness. On my mother's heart," she said, resting her hand over that precious organ she'd just mentioned.

"I just don't want to disappoint you guys," I said, as though nothing was private or sacred anymore. All my insecurities had been exposed over a plate of chocolate cake and a glass of milk. Who knew that was all it took to extract everything out of me that had been haunting me for what felt like a lifetime. The worry over disappointing my parents, this guilt building up inside of me—for years—that if I didn't pick the family business of *Anderson and Sons*, I'd be disowned, or considered a disappointment. But it all melted away when I looked at the sincere eyes staring back at me with nothing but an earnest love in them. Maybe my mom knew what she was talking about all along. Maybe love did prevail.

"And, honey, Laurel is so young. You both are. And she has a lot of grief she's going to have to sort out and unfortunately live with and try to navigate her way through the thick of it. All you can do is be there for her. There's no one like your mom, and after losing her mom the way she did…" Mom sighed, closed her eyes, and had a moment of pain flash across her face before she continued. "Well, I'll just say I wouldn't wish that hurt on anyone, let alone someone so young."

"What do you mean? How did she lose her?" Her statement tore me away from my own thoughts.

"You know her mom was under the care of hospice, right?" Mom asked.

"I'd heard something like that in passing." I nodded my head. "I heard she had cancer."

"I wasn't her mother's nurse, but the hospice I work for provided her care. And you know I work closely with Pam, who was Laurel's mom's hospice nurse."

My eyebrows scrunched up together. I wasn't sure what was going to come out the other end of this conversation.

"Laurel's mom did have cancer, but that's not what she died from."

"I don't understand. Then what did she die from?"

"Laurel's mom had a very rare form of brain cancer that was aggressive. When she was diagnosed, she was given a year or less to live. Brain cancer has a way of altering so much. We lose a lot of ourselves in the process. It causes hallucinations, and from day to day, it can be hard to decipher reality from things that aren't real. And that can be terrifying for both the patient and the families."

"I see," I heard myself say under my breath. I didn't know what this was leading up to.

"She waited until one morning, after having planned this out for some time, for Laurel and her dad to go out on some errand, insisting that she was fine—which at the time she was—and she left them a note. Pam got a phone call from Laurel's mom right beforehand. And Pam asked me to go out with her so she wouldn't be alone. I'll never, ever forget that day."

"Mom…"

"She killed herself. Laurel's mom committed suicide."

SASHA HIBBS

Chapter Nineteen

The Ides of March

Laurel

"Well, Zelda is an older dog, but for all intents and purposes, she appears to be healthy," the vet said, leaning back up to look at me and Dad as he completed his examination on her. I had been anxious for weeks wondering what the small lump on her abdomen was.

"And what about the lump?" Dad asked, as though reading my mind.

"I'd say it's just a fatty tumor, and nine out of ten times those are benign and nothing to worry about," the vet said.

"But what if it's not?" I spoke up, my stomach tied in knots at the thought of my sweet girl possibly being sick or worse, in pain.

With a small sigh escaping under his breath, the vet pushed his glasses up the bridge of his nose and crossed his arms as though in contemplation of how best to answer my hard question. "Zelda is eleven years old. That's a nice long life for a German Shepherd. I never make any guarantees about my patients coming out the other end of surgery awake, alive, *or* okay. But in her case, she's at a significantly increased risk of not making it out of the operating room period."

I could've puked as he said this so matter-of-factly about my girl, my childhood pet that was so much more than a pet. Zelda was everything that was good, gentle, and innocent.

"If it were me personally, I'd enjoy the rest of her time—however long that may be—and watch and wait. If there are any additional symptoms that develop like she stops eating, drinking, painful movement, or no bowel movements, I want you to call my office, and we will come up with a plan from there."

I looked down into Zelda's soft brown eyes, and my heart broke at the thought of losing her. She seemed to sense my distress like she always did, and she leaned into me to provide the comfort she so selflessly always gave.

"So, in your opinion, even if she'd need the tumor removed, you wouldn't recommend her having surgery?" Dad asked, repeating the vet's assessment.

The vet shook his head. "Not at her age. No."

"But you say there's a good chance this is nothing to worry about?" Dad asked.

"Without a biopsy there's no one hundred percent way of me knowing anything. And we can biopsy, but that will only rule out or confirm, but ultimately not change my recommendation on how to treat her. Do you want me to biopsy the area?"

Dad looked at me and down to Zelda, and then back up to the vet. "No."

"Okay. Again, if anything new develops, call my office."

"Come on, girl," Dad said to Zelda, giving her a gentle stroke between the ears.

We stopped by the receptionist desk to pay our balance and schedule a follow-up for June.

On the car ride home, Zelda sat up front with us, between me and my dad with her head in my lap. I ran my hands through her soft fur, and I could feel the gentle rise and fall of her breathing. She was content.

I couldn't imagine a world without Zelda in it, and so I wasn't going to. I couldn't. I just couldn't. She was only eleven. German Shepherds had lived to be much older than that. Aside from the small lump on her abdomen she was healthy. She ate, drank, played, walked all over the property, still slept in bed with me. She was going to be fine. I believed it in my heart. She had to be. I *needed* her to be.

"Are you nervous for your audition?" Dad asked, which was a nice distraction from my worry over Zelda, but it brought on another level of anxiety—Braydon.

"It's only the first audition, but yes, I guess a little," I answered, looking out the window while continuing to stroke Zelda, which was comforting for us both.

"You guess? It's a pretty big deal. I had no doubt my girl would be invited to audition. Me and your mom always knew this day would come. And of all the schools, you hit the jackpot! But why the sad face?"

I had no idea how he could see anything from the angle we were both at. Maybe it was parental intuition that let him see the worry on my face. "I haven't told Brayden yet."

"Oh, I see." There was a minute of silence that stretched on between us. "A penny for your thoughts?"

"I'm not even really sure what I'm thinking," I answered truthfully. I could hardly assimilate my thoughts and feelings into a cohesive formula that made any sense.

"Well, I can definitely see you're bothered when what you should be is happy. Being invited to audition for a scholarship with Berklee of all places is no small feat. And if you haven't told Brayden therein lies the problem. You have some hesitancy *because*...?" He trailed off, and I knew he was trying to lead me to the threshold of my own mind versus putting words in my mouth.

My mind was racing, my thoughts so clouded. I *should* be happy, excited actually, to be invited to audition for the school of my dreams because lord knows there were several hoops I had to jump through to even get to this stage, but I suppose when I was able to sort through all the clouds and fog, I could clearly see Braydon at the other end. And it led me to another bridge I had to eventually cross that I didn't want to.

Us.

What should I do about the two of us? When I talked to Brayden about what things looked like after graduation for him, he seemed adamant on taking up the family business and staying here. And nothing was wrong with here. It was home. But Czar and Buckhannon also wasn't Boston where Berklee was. And did long distance relationships ever really work out? I hoped. I wanted that. I wanted to believe. I wanted Brayden. He was everything that was different from me. He played football. I played piano. He was popular. I was homeschooled most of my life. There were enough charming opposites between us that everything about him just felt … *right*.

But yet in the very back of my mind there was this tiny seed of doubt, and every time I went to apply a mental weed killer, it seemed to take hold even stronger, refusing to die. I could only ignore my doubts so long before knowing that I had to eventually face them.

"He wants to stay here," I answered.

"And?"

"I don't know how we will work out apart, long distance."

"I see," Dad said, his gaze on the road. "Well, I think the idea is if you and he are meant to be, you simply work whether you are together in one state, or not."

"I guess."

"He's not going to college? I thought maybe he'd parlayed his football into a sports scholarship, like he could play at Davis and Elkins College or Wesleyan."

"No, he seems hellbent on working with his dad at his dad's business."

"There's nothing wrong with that if that's what he wants to do."

"I get that. And I know. I do. I think maybe I'm just feeling overwhelmed."

"One thing at a time, honey. One thing at a time."

I knew my dad was trying to be helpful, but a car ride wasn't going to resolve my doubts. Ultimately, something had to give. As I scratched Zelda between her ears, I figured for now I'd enjoy what was given to me— the rest of the school year. I'd worry about the future when it came at me.

SASHA HIBBS

Chapter Twenty

April Showers

Brayden

"You ever think about what it's like not here?" I asked Chase as I shoved my drenched coat in a locker I rarely used. I almost forgot the combination.

"In school?"

"Yeah, no, I mean, like have you ever thought about going to college out of state?"

"Bruh, we're seniors and ready to graduate like next month. It's a little late in the game don't you think?" Chase laughed at me.

"I mean, I guess. But I don't know if anything is really too late, is it?"

"Dude, I've already been accepted into Wesleyan. My dad went there. His dad went there. My parents would kill me if I went anywhere else."

We walked toward the auditorium. Laurel had told me she had an appointment today and would miss.

"Yeah, I get that, but have you ever thought about going anywhere else?"

"Nah, not really." Chase shoved the doors open to the auditorium and I followed behind him. We both plopped down in some seats in the back row. "Man, where's this coming from? You having thoughts about going to college? I thought you were going to go into business with your dad? And doesn't that require like some kind of license too?"

"I don't know, man," I said, more under my breath than anything. The struggle within was becoming more and more real. "I guess I really don't know what I want to do. I'd always just assumed staying here is what I'd do, and I was always fine with that until—"

"Laurel," Chase said, cutting me off.

I just glanced at him and then gazed absentmindedly at the stage, kind of daydreaming of her up there performing.

"But are you second guessing all this shit because Laurel may be going off somewhere or because you want to go to college out of state? Dude, like how did you even do on the SATs?"

Chase was chattering beside me, but my thoughts trailed off thinking about things he brought up. Did I even want to go to college? What did I want to do past high school? Did I want to work with my dad? Did I want to leave the state? Stay?

No.

What I wanted was Laurel.

And as the days passed and graduation loomed over the both of us like a cloud of doom threatening to take her away from me, like that malevolent storm cloud, my mood grew and grew and grew. I didn't know what to do or which way to turn. I wanted somehow to turn back the hand of time, go back to the beginning of summer when those first notes hit my ears all those months ago. No. I'd go back even farther. To know Laurel and I had been in the same school for this entire time, and I had paid no attention to her … what an idiot I'd been.

There were guest speakers today from various colleges, and normally I would've drifted off to sleep in the back row somewhere, but instead everything around me faded out while my mind raced on all things Laurel. Chase was even beside me talking. I nodded to him occasionally, but I heard nothing. I saw nothing. There might as well have been no one on the stage but Laurel, a piano, and cascading lights surrounding her. And me off to the side wondering how to hold onto her.

****

Chase and I walked out of the auditorium after being dismissed. Somewhere along the way we parted ways. I didn't really hear what he was saying, and there was a remote part of me that felt bad for that, but the majority of myself, the part that seemed in control currently, didn't care either.

As I walked down the hall, I looked up and saw Laurel standing by the advisor's office. I stopped and backed up against the wall so she wouldn't see me. She'd told me she had an appointment today, but I hadn't asked with whom. I assumed maybe a doctor's appointment, or I didn't know, really. But I trusted if it was something I needed to know, she'd tell me. But here I was in the hallway thinking she wasn't even in school today, and she was standing outside the advisor's door clearly waiting for him. And the only reason as a senior you had an appointment with him was to talk about college plans.

My head was spinning.

I felt sick.

Why?

I knew this was coming.

Knew it was a possibility.

So why was I freaking out?

Because she was going to leave, and when she left there was nothing that could be done about having to leave me behind.

I flicked my gaze outside. It was April. How much time did that give me? Months? Weeks? Less?

It was dumping the rain down. Never had I felt so in tune with the weather in all my life. I felt gray inside. I also felt this storm, a storm of something rolling in, closing in on me. And there was this remote part in the back of my brain clawing at me, this feeling that somehow, she'd betrayed me.

SASHA HIBBS

Chapter Twenty-One

Lying About the Truth

Laurel

Getting into Berklee was going to be nothing short of a miracle. The admission process was rigid, tuition was pricey, and the competition for a scholarship was stiff. We didn't have money, so my only option if I wanted to get into Berklee was to win the coveted scholarship which made the already stiff competition pretty much like going up against an impenetrable brick wall. But I'd dreamed of this my entire life. And step one was to obtain an invitation. I held said invitation in my hands, an invitation that I'd just presented to the jury, a panel of jurors consisting of admission personnel and actual instructors. I didn't know any of them, but they all looked intimidating to me.

They were holding auditions in Clarksburg at the Robinson Grand, this super cool vintage theater restored to its former 1913 glory. Somehow the grandeur of the place made me feel that much smaller, like I was a poor girl raised up a West Virginia holler and I just came down off the mountain with my pa and hound dog, and to a limited degree, that was true.

"Ms. Bennett, the piano is ready for you," a lady looking down her nose through large glasses said to me. Her hair was secured in the tightest bun I'd ever seen. There wasn't a bit of humor in the hard lines on her face, only a look of 'nothing impresses me, but you, like all the others, are welcome to try'."

My father was sitting in the very back. I knew he was there and that was enough encouragement for me. Him and my mom were my biggest fans and supporters my entire life. I had some idea of what they'd sacrificed so I could have musical equipment—which wasn't cheap—so I could be exposed to every possible learning opportunity out there. They went without so I didn't have to.

But my mom was gone, and I owed it to my dad's many years of sacrificing to give this round one of auditions all I could. Scary judgmental elitist lady or not, I had to do this.

I took a deep breath and placed one foot in front of the other, each step up the cold polished floor making a loud clunk underneath my nervous footing.

Once I reached the piano, I gently lowered myself onto the bench.

I thought of my mama. I closed my eyes and allowed my fingertips to run over the keys. Behind my eyes burst a memory of my younger self sitting next to my mama playing her favorite tune, *Fur Elise* by Beethoven. My fingertips lived out that memory, that ability to never forget, and there was something special, some passionate hurt that came across in my playing, knowing the familiar old tune wasn't enough. I played that familiar old tune like someone you loved and then lost, just like my mother could hear from beyond the grave if only I played a certain way. I knew this deep sense of hurt was coming out in my playing. I could just feel the hum of it permeating the air.

I took my time playing—a dedication to my mother's memory. I tried so hard to keep the tears at bay, but try as I may, they came anyway. This was my mother—the music, the soulfulness, the tears. They were all like roses I was throwing up on a stage for her memory, just as she did for me when alive. When I finally hit the final key, only then did I open my watery eyes to silence.

It was deafening.

Finally, I stood up and faced my panel of judges.

Intense lady gave me a scrutinizing look, one that seemed to stretch on forever before she finally leaned in toward her microphone. "While Fur Elise was a very predictable move…"

My heart sank.

"I might add that you played it with unusual vigor, which is a compliment to you."

I let out the breath I'd been holding.

"To whom, young lady, were you playing that for?"

I tried to gain control of my voice, but it was still shaky when I answered. "My mother."

"Is she here in the audience today?" she asked with an arched eyebrow.

"No."

"Hmmm, pity."

"She passed away."

"I see," she said, and I detected the smallest change in her voice. "You'll have our decision within two months whether or not you will advance."

They all took down notes, never making eye contact with me and leaving me with no indication of how well or poor I'd done. It was unnerving.

"Thank you," I said, lowering my head and walking off the stage into the darkness of the back, looking for my dad. I instantly felt better once I saw his smiling face.

"That's my girl! Your mom would've been so proud. I know I sure am. How about we go celebrate with some ice cream?"

That sounded like the most childish thing in the world and also the best. There were times I wished I were that little child again, just me, my mom, my dad, Zelda, all of us together, happy and whole where my biggest problem in life was picking out what flavor of ice cream I wanted. Now, it seemed like every step was riddled with problems.

"That sounds wonderful."

As we rode to the Dairy Duchess two things were weighing me down—the sad look in Zelda's eyes as she laid her head in my lap, and the guilt I felt for having not told Brayden about my audition.

I longed for a simpler time, a time when I wasn't plagued with guilt, a time when Zelda was younger, because I knew in my heart our girl was sick.

****

"I'm gonna miss you," Emily said, throwing a pillow at me.

I caught it and threw it right back. "I don't even know if I've made it to the final audition. That was just the first one."

"Hey, you got the golden ticket, and I know you killed it. I have no doubt, and since I'm always right, you'll be getting that second and final one. Then you'll find out you've won a scholarship, and you'll move to Boston, and it'll be forever before I see you again. You'll be famous and that will be that."

"I'd buy us a condo in Hatteras. We'd vacation there. You'd have to come live with me. Can you imagine? Me traveling with the Berklee Orchestra?" I was dreaming, and it was a beautiful dream. "Dad and Zelda, too."

"Not Brayden?" Emily asked, sitting up on her bed, crossing her legs absentmindedly.

"I don't know," I answered, my thoughts taking a turn back in the same direction I kept running from.

"Laurel?" Emily said, arching a suspecting brow at me.

"Yes?"

"Have you told Brayden if you get a scholarship to Berklee, you're going to move there?" Emily asked, but I could tell by the way she drew out her question slowly, she'd already surmised I hadn't.

"I haven't really told Brayden about Berklee. When we first started dating, his brother mentioned Juilliard and wanted to know if I had plans of attending out of state, but it was a passing comment and I've kind of dodged the topic altogether."

"And?"

"And what?"

"And is that it? Haven't you told him anything else?"

"No, I guess not," I answered. The feeling of letting the truth out versus holding it in made my mind feel at peace.

"But why? What are you afraid of?"

I took a deep breath and closed my eyes. In that brief moment between closing my eyes and the silence surrounding it, was a pure clarity, a simple truth that was battering at my brain, as though begging to be released from its mental prison.

I opened my eyes and looked at my cousin, my lifelong friend, one of the people I loved most in the world. "I'm afraid of things changing, of not being as they are now."

Emily looked at me for what felt like several seconds contemplating what I'd just confessed before speaking. "Pap always says the truth comes out in the end, but maybe it should come out before then. Maybe telling Brayden how you really feel—"

"I just don't know what to say or how to say it," I said, cutting her off.

She gave me a look of consideration.

"Aren't you agonizing over what to do about you

and Chase?"

"Why?" she asked, scrunching her eyebrows up. "Why would I?"

"Well, I mean he's going to Wesleyan and you're going to West Liberty three hours away. Like how is that supposed to work?"

"Like however it works," Emily answered. "I'm not worried about it. Things will work out how they are meant to work out. I'm worried about graduating high school right now, not college or boyfriends or what life looks like in the next five years. I'm worried about right now."

"I wish I were that way."

"My only wish is for you to be happy."

I knew happiness. I loved happiness. But I also understood how happiness was a fickle being. Happiness would be with you one minute, and then like that last breath, happiness could leave you without notice. I wanted Brayden. I wanted Berklee. I wanted everything. And it felt like one would cancel out the other.

I still had a few months. Maybe I should take Emily's advice and worry about today, worry about right now, because in the end I knew tomorrow wasn't promised.

Chapter Twenty-Two

Fishing in the Dark

Brayden

"Fishing?" Laurel asked, a bit surprised and humored at my request. "And at nighttime?"

"Well sure, it's an Appalachian rite of passage," I said, while grinning at her.

"I've got to say as long as I've lived here, I have never fished, let alone at night, but if you say it's a requirement of our people, well who am I to argue tradition?" she said with a playful tone in her voice that encouraged me, made me feel at ease. I was worried she'd think this was stupid.

"Exactly," I said, pulling her into me and resting my chin on top of her head. "So, I'll pick you up in a few hours? That will give me time to go home, grab some poles, tackle and bait, and come back for you. We will go to Stonecoal Lake. That's a great spot."

"Cool, cool," she said, slowly pulling away from me. "Thanks for dropping me off. I'll be ready. You'll be here around…" She looked down at her watch and then back up to me. "Seven o'clock?"

"Yeah, it gets dark by seven-thirty, so that will give us time to get there and find a good spot before it gets dark."

I grabbed her again real quick and kissed her. She relaxed in my arms, and I was sad to let her go. "Be back soon."

I saw Zelda laying on the porch as I watched Laurel walk up to go inside. Zelda was usually right by her side, and she was always happy to see me, but she was looking old and tired these days. But Laurel never said anything about her. I watched them both disappear behind the door and once she closed it, I got in my truck and drove home.

****

"Here, you better take this," Mom said from behind me. I was in the garage packing up poles, chairs, tackle, all the things needed to fish. I turned around to see her holding a basket.

"You'll get hungry for some food later, I'm sure," she said, handing me over what I knew was some good snacks. My mom always made the best food.

"Gawd, thank you, Mom!"

"Of course. There're some chicken salad croissants, cherry pie made with those sweet ones you like, some sweet tea in mason jars so they don't spill, and you'll also need to take a blanket in case it gets cold. Summer might be around the corner, but it's not here yet and the nights can get pretty chilly. The last thing you or Laurel need is a cold."

"You are the best, seriously," I said.

"Where are you guys going?"

"Stonecoal Lake."

"That's a good spot. You be the gentleman I raised you to be and have fun and be careful," she said as she reached up on her tiptoes giving me a kiss on the cheek.

"Yes, ma'am."

"I'll leave the porch light on for you."

"Thanks, Mom."

"Maybe you'll get lucky enough to see fireflies tonight. It's getting to be that time of year."

"I hope so."

****

Laurel was waiting for me on her deck. I smiled at the sight of her. She was wearing jeans and a green checkered flannel and had her hair in two loose braids, and she never looked prettier to me. Her dad appeared behind her shortly after I parked the truck.

"Laurel says you're going night fishing."

"Yes, sir. At Stonecoal Lake. I think there's enough service there if you need to call or you need to reach Laurel," I said, walking onto the deck. Her dad was the nicest guy, but he was still her dad and every time I came to pick her up, I felt like I was being low-key scrutinized. I guess that's what dads did.

"Well, you two be safe and have fun. Good luck."

"Love you, Dad," Laurel said, hugging her dad quickly before falling in step beside me.

"See you later, Scott." I waved bye and opened the truck door for Laurel.

Stonecoal was only about a twenty-minute drive from her house. She popped in a disc of Creedence Clearwater Revival—another band I was unfamiliar with until meeting Laurel—and hummed a tune under her breath.

There was so much that hung between us. But for now, at this moment, I just wanted to enjoy the truck ride with Laurel. I wanted to keep glancing over at her looking out the window, the setting sun casting a special kind of soft light against her profile, hearing the faintest beauty of her voice as she sang along with some kind of folky rock ballad, and the contentment I felt of being in her presence. If I could capture and bottle a moment up, it would've been that truck ride.

I pulled down a narrow gravel road that led to the part of the lake the public could access. "You're in for a treat."

"Oh yeah?"

"Mmhmm. Night fishing is pretty magical." I pulled over and out of the way, then put the truck in park. Night fishing to me was a wonderful escape. I'd always loved the tranquility of moonlit waters, how thrilling it could be to navigate the darkness, and the strategy you had to employ to fish in the dark. But something about Laurel being here, experiencing the magic of it with me, made me more excited than the actual act of fishing.

I left the CD on. The battery could be left on for a while before it made the truck dead. I just had to start it every now and then. I loved that she was nostalgic and wanted to listen to CDs versus playing music through our phones. That must've been something she picked up from her parents.

I grabbed our chairs from the back. "Stay put. I'll be right back. Let me find a spot real quick and set up these chairs. Then I'll grab our poles."

"Cool," she said, smiling and then resuming humming whatever tune was playing.

I only had to go about twenty feet before finding a place level and dry enough that I could also throw our blanket out. I set the chairs up and went back to the truck. I pulled our poles out of the bed and walked back around to Laurel's door. "Would you mind grabbing the basket? Mom packed us something to eat."

"That was sweet of her! I swear you have the nicest mom."

"Yeah, she's okay, I guess," I said, smiling at her.

Laurel lowered herself from the truck with the basket and blanket.

I grabbed the poles and tackle. Then I asked her to follow me. "Here's our spot. The music can still play, but not too loudly or we will scare off the fish."

"Hmmm … gotcha, gotcha. So, you don't want me busting out my guitar and jamming?"

"Well, I'm sure the fish wouldn't mind getting serenaded, maybe even after they hear you, we can use your voice as bait," I said, playfully tapping my chin in thought.

"So, show me how this 'night fishing' works," Laurel said. "And it's important that you know I'm grossed out by worms."

"Well, it's pretty hard stuff. First, we have to put our blanket down," I said, laying the poles down on the ground and spreading out the blanket beside our chairs. "And then, you have to place your bait exactly right when you hook it, and good thing I already was aware of your distaste for worms, so we have fake bait."

"I never told you that. How did you know I'm terrified of worms?"

"I asked your dad," I said with a smile. "So, I guess I won't put any down your shirt."

"That has to be about the most boyish thing I've ever heard you say, and I promise, you do that, and you won't hear me sing, you, all the fish, and anyone in ear shot will hear me scream."

"On my honor," I said, placing a dramatic hand across my chest. I baited our fishing poles and started casting the lines out. "Like this." I gently casted into the water. I could hear the familiar 'plop' and then I reeled the line in just enough to give me some rope should we get a bite.

"And now what?" she said, looking between me and the water.

"And now we wait, or better yet, we eat."

"Well, if this is a sport, I could get used to this."

"Yeah, it's really not that bad."

"So, what is it that you like about night fishing?" Laurel asked while she lowered herself down on the blanket, emptying the contents of my mother's picnic basket.

I thought about it briefly as I sat down close to her. I gazed out into the quiet water and took in the beginning beams of the moon lit up against the watery darkness. "I love the quiet. But I also love the sounds made in the quiet. I love hearing the katydids, the occasional croaking of a frog, or a frog jumping into the water, the hum of the nightlife—all the bugs even—the lapping of the water against the riverbank, the sounds the trees make when a breeze blows in." I felt like I was rattling on and on. But when I gave her a sideways glance all I saw was beautiful Laurel listening intently. "I guess you could say I really don't care much about the actual fishing part."

"I think I understand. Sometimes the sounds made in silence are the most clarifying, like everything, all the chaos and nonsense of our daily lives just somehow fades away in the calm, and clarity surfaces. That's how I feel when I'm walking in the woods with Zelda. I kind of feel that here with you now," she said softly, her gaze holding some kind of special something that I couldn't quite identify.

"Yes, that's it exactly," I said, my voice low and impassioned. Laurel was so special. She seemed to understand thoughts and feelings beyond what I could ever put into words. And I could, even in the dark, see that in her eyes when she looked at me. I swallowed hard and tried to refocus. "You're going to love my mom's cherry pie."

"So," she began, and I could hear her try to clear her voice as well, "do you ever actually catch any fish?"

"Oh, sure. But I usually unhook them and put them back in if I do." I removed the Saran wrap from the cherry pie and handed her a piece.

She accepted and took a bite. "Oh, this *is* good."

"Told you," I said, smiling as I bit down into my own piece.

"You know, this kind of reminds me a little bit of when my parents would take me to the beach. My dad would jury into an art show, and we'd go for the show, but also attach a small vacation to it as well. I loved the less crowded beaches, and they'd take me down to the shore at night when it was dark, and no one was really out—except all the crabs. There were crabs everywhere."

"Really? I wonder why?" I asked.

"Dad always said it was because it was cooler at night and with less predators, but I don't really know, I never looked it up. But this is similar." She paused for a moment and looked over her shoulder toward the water and then back to me. "And it's nice. Calming."

From my periphery, the faintest flickering neon light caught my attention. It must've Laurel's too because she turned her gaze at the same time as me and let out an excited sigh. "Fireflies! I love fireflies."

"Mom said we might see some. I wasn't sure if it was too early in the season for them." I watched a couple dart around us, but mostly watched Laurel's fascination with them.

"Do you want to know what my mama said the truth about fireflies is?" she said, while extending her hand in time for one of those luminous beauties to land on her fingertips.

"Sure," I said, tilting my head back in time to see another firefly light up past me and then flee into the night.

"Well, most people know the reason a firefly lights up is because of bioluminescence and attracting a potential mate. However, Mama said there was a bit more to it than simple science. She always said matters of the heart involved the soul too." Laurel looked down at the firefly in her hand, extending it up higher so it would fly off, free. "Fireflies have a specific way of shining their light. She always said in order for them to attract the right mate, they flash theirs in an exact pattern—a love pattern—and only the right soulmate responds. And so, after finding their soulmate, should they be parted, they will always recognize that light, that pattern, and therefore can always find their way back to each other."

"Laurel?"

"Mmhmm," she murmured under her breath in a dreamy state.

"When I first heard you sing that night, it was like this."

"What do you mean?"

"It was quiet, or I should say everything else around you was quiet," I said, and I could see she looked a bit perplexed. "What I mean to say is that once I heard you sing and play your guitar it didn't matter that it was on Main Street. It didn't matter that there were cars and motorcycles, and other people coming and going, and there were all kinds of noises floating around. It was like here, right now, fishing in the dark, with nothing else but fireflies lighting the way. I heard you and everything else around me went still. It was only you. And I don't know if I ever told you, but I went home that night and watched every uploaded video of you I could find. I'd never heard or seen anything so, so, so…" I was struggling to find the one word that would describe what Laurel meant to me in my heart. "…enchanting, so magical, so beautiful. Your voice is like that beautiful silence and the clarity that follows, like night fishing—"

She cut me off by quickly wrapping her arms around my waist, causing me to lose my balance so that we were lying down, she being stretched out on top of me. She lowered her lips to mine and kissed me like every emotion she felt could only be conveyed in a kiss, like it was the most important thing she could do.

I was powerless to do anything but wrap my arms around her, pulling her closer into me. She invaded everything, every inch of me. She smelled like clean linen, like the sheets my mom pulled off the clothesline. Her lips were soft and hungry, as though she couldn't kiss me harder or fast enough. Soon, her legs slid in between mine and I felt a heat sear in the pit of my stomach, and it gravitated toward my groin. My head was getting light, light, lighter. My hands started to navigate downward, over her shoulders, to her waistline, down to her soft buttocks. I rolled her over, continuing to kiss her lips, and then her throat, her stomach.

"Laurel…" I looked up at her heated gaze, pleading with my eyes for her to stop me, yet praying she'd let me continue at the same time.

She pulled me back down to her. And I was lost. Somewhere in the heat of our touch, I'd unbuttoned her flannel while she pulled my shirt over my head. She was wearing a black bra that exposed a fair amount of her breasts.

I'd never gone this far with a girl before. But Laurel wasn't just any girl.

She was sunshine.

She was clarity.

She was everything I wanted.

She was everything I needed.

And nothing could've stopped me in that moment but a light of clarity, of truth. Somehow remembering that I loved her too much to take her virginity and give her mine prevailed against raging hormones. And it was the fireflies that darted behind her, lighting up her beauty that was even more so in this aroused state, that made me float back gently to earth.

"Laurel," I croaked out, a swarm of frogs in my throat. "I'm sorry." I shook my head, trying to clear the remnants of lust and love back down to a manageable point.

She leaned back, buttoning her flannel back up. "It's okay. I got carried away too…" Her voice trailed off as her phone laid haphazardly beside us lit up several notifications. She grabbed it and I could see the lines on her face become thin with worry.

"What's wrong?" I asked, while pulling my shirt down over my head.

"I had my phone on silent and missed like ten calls from my dad. I don't know if I have enough service out here to get his voicemails, if he left any."

I could easily hear the worry in her voice. "We better go."

We silently agreed, quickly packing and loading up the truck. I could see the worry in her quick pace, in the way she threw everything together without a care. And I was worried for her. I couldn't imagine what her dad would be blowing her phone up for, what couldn't wait until she got home, or why, if it were so important to call her a million times, he didn't just drive out to get her. I told him plainly where we were.

And this would be yet another time among many that I looked back and felt I failed Laurel miserably.

The silence we rode to her house in was broken the minute we pulled up in her driveway and her father walked out to meet her.

"Honey, you got here just in time," Scott said.

"What do you mean?" It was dark, but somehow, I could see all the color drain from Laurel's face.

"I tried to call you. I was afraid to leave her to come get you, afraid if I did, she'd go alone. And I couldn't move her."

Laurel let out a bellow so full of anguish it ripped my heart, a tear like a loose thread that was just beginning to unravel.

"No!" she screamed, running into her house, me

behind her.

Once inside, I moved out of the way so Scott could get past me. Curled up on their couch was her childhood dog, Zelda, so weak she couldn't lift her head, but instead, the minute Laurel was by her side, she lifted her gaze to what she loved most in this world—the girl she grew up with. The girl who loved her. The girl who slept beside her like sisters having to share a bed for the last twelve years. The girl who talked to her as though she was human, because looking at those wise brown eyes, it was a struggle for me to believe she was otherwise.

And sure enough, what Scott said proved to be true. Somehow, that beautiful soul had waited on the girl she loved most before leaving them forever. She looked up to Laurel, and Laurel curled up beside her, telling her it was okay, that she was loved, and with one last audible sigh, she closed her eyes forever.

SASHA HIBBS

Chapter Twenty-Three

The Death of a Childhood

Laurel

There was a sort of curse that came along with the ability to remember everything through touch because there were times I'd give anything to simply forget, to live in a world of amnesia. As I curled myself up against Zelda and ran my fingers through her soft black coat, every childhood memory seared up my arm and burst behind my eyelids. And my heart was shattered because as she took her last breath all I was left with were memories as vivid as though they happened yesterday.

I was so little, maybe four when our little family went to pick her out, but I remembered exactly what the day was like. Mom and Dad drove us to a little bee farm in Morgantown where this farmer kept bees, sold honey, and also had black German Shepherds. I remembered it was sunny, springtime, and I could smell all the flowers coming into bloom. We walked up to the pin containing what looked like several black furballs, and the farmer let them loose. They all went crazy, and my four-year-old self was in heaven as they shot in between my ankles, rolled over on their backs, gave their best little barks.

All except one.

Our Zelda.

She'd been waiting on us. She shyly padded over to my dad and plopped down on the tip of his boot and looked over her shoulder and up at him with her big brown saucer eyes, and it was over.

We'd loved her every day since and she us. She loved us through hard times. She loved us through the best of times. She loved us through my mother's death, got me through many nights of crying myself to sleep.

She'd nose her way under my arm, wedging herself between me and my pillow as though to say, *You can always cry on my shoulder*.

And she never asked for anything in return. All she wanted to do from that day so many years ago on the farm until she took her last breath was just to give us all of her love.

"Sweetheart, we are going to have to bury her," I heard my father say from somewhere in the room. My head felt so foggy. I just couldn't bring myself to lift my head, to look at her dead body because it would be real then and I didn't want that. Didn't want any part of that. My instinct was to cling to her tighter.

"Honey—"

"No! We should've taken her to another vet! No! No! No!" I screamed as loud as I could, crying harder and harder, my chest burning and throbbing.

"Laurel, you listen to me, Zelda was twelve. She lived a long life. We both wanted her longer. She was too old to withstand that kind of surgery. She deserved to die here with those she loved instead of on an operating table."

"I didn't want her longer. I wanted her forever!" I felt sick in my stomach, an all too familiar ache from crying so hard, crying so hard I could throw up.

"Laurel, come here. Laurel," my dad said from somewhere behind me.

I felt his hand on my shoulder, and I gently jerked away from him. If he took Zelda away, it would be forever. I'd never see her again, only in a memory that never faded, memories that tormented me for being so real, and yet the ones I loved so dearly in them were slowly leaving me.

"Laurel, this must be done. Zelda was a good girl. She loved us. She waited to say her goodbyes. Now we have to do right by her and place her by the other one we love the most."

I sobbed and sobbed, knowing full well he meant to bury Zelda by my mother. My mother who was also dead. This time when he placed his hand on my shoulder, I didn't jerk away.

I slowly lifted my head and eased myself up, the gravity, the reality, the overwhelming sadness hitting me over and over again at what must be done.

I stood up—my face felt so swollen—and I looked over at Brayden. I wasn't ashamed to cry. Zelda was worthy of every tear and so much more. But pain was hard to display. It was so personal, so private.

His gaze held so many unspoken things. And really, I couldn't fault him. I could imagine being in his shoes, unsure of what to say, how to console someone in so much grief.

"Laurel, I—" Brayden began, but I cut him off.

"Thank you for bringing me home. I'll text you later."

"I can stay," he said, hands in pocket. He looked uncomfortable. I'm sure he was.

"No, that's okay. Really, it's okay."

"I'll be looking for your text," he said almost sheepishly, and without another moment, he jetted out the door.

The private part of me that felt this was pain shared only between my dad and I was relieved he was gone. And the other part of me that let Brayden in our private world felt abandoned, almost betrayed that he'd go so easily, so quickly without a fight.

Dad placed a blanket over her gently. "Come with me."

I followed my dad to that old familiar battle ground. The resting place of my mother and his wife, the battle welling up inside of me to not relive her death every time I came here to talk to her. And now we'd be adding my precious Zelda to this resting place, this sacred ground that held parts of my heart within its bosom. I wondered in this moment how much grief one could withstand.

I glanced over at my dad, and I could see tears well up in his eyes and that nearly broke me, knowing I wasn't the only one grieving, that my father's heart was just as broken. He dug a few shovels full of dirt before handing me the shovel.

Part of this shared pain was exercising the grief. Opening up the earth to place one of the souls we loved most into it was sacred, a sort of ritual needed to begin the healing process. As I shoveled, I felt the soft pelting of cold rain against my skin.

I was grateful to the universe for the rain. It was as though the world cried with us, and it made me hate the universe a little less.

Once her grave was dug, I watched my father gingerly gather her up in his arms and lower her to the resting place below. As we took turns shoveling in dirt, I sang the one song that encompassed what Zelda meant to me.

With nothing but the beating of the rain for music, I sang *You Are My Sunshine*, and I prayed to whatever was out there that my Zelda could hear my words and believe them in her heart. I prayed that she felt loved.

"You always made me happy, Zelda. Even when the skies were gray."

I kissed my fingertips and gently laid my hand against the mound that contained our beautiful girl.

How would I ever make it through this?

Chapter Twenty-Four

Marching to the Beat

Brayden

Time seemed to be like me trying to hold water—it was just slipping through my hands. I didn't know why I felt like I was up against some kind of internal clock, and it was constantly ticking, chasing me like a hellhound on my ass. But to what? To what end? To what doom? I couldn't quite put my finger on it, but I felt it, nonetheless.

I was getting worried about Laurel. She missed a few days of school and hadn't answered any of my texts. I finally got in touch with Emily and found out she'd stayed there for a long weekend. I guess she didn't have to run that by me. I was just a little surprised she never mentioned it, that she never answered any of my texts.

I wandered into the kitchen and started going through the cupboards, looking for anything to eat when my mom, with her uncanny mother ability, came around the corner. She had a sixth sense, I swear it. She always seemed to know when something deep down was bothering me, and she always was able to produce some kind of insane sweet to comfort me with.

"It's not German chocolate cake, but I do have some leftover carrot cake I brought home from our covered dish event at work. Could I interest you in a piece and also perhaps ask about your thoughts?" she asked, already plating up a slice for me.

"Thanks, Mom." I took the cake she offered and sat at the kitchen table. I could feel her gaze on me, as she waited for an answer. But I didn't know what to say. I wasn't sure how to put into words what I was feeling. Again, with her uncanny sense of things, she began.

"How is Laurel doing? I've not seen her for what seems like several days, and while I am glad, who I have seen is *you*."

I swallowed a bite of cake and took a deep sigh. "I've not heard from her in a few days, but I know she's staying at her cousin, Emily's, house."

"Uh huh. I see, I see," she said, grabbing a second fork and taking a bite of my cake. "The two of you have been pretty attached at the hip. Seems a little odd to me that suddenly you're not. I feel like there might be something you're not telling me. And it's okay if you don't want to. Just know that I'm here to listen if you need to talk to someone."

I mulled over her words. I did want to say something, but I didn't know what, didn't quite know how to get it out because I knew somewhere buried deep, something was bothering me, but I didn't know how to identify it.

Seeming to sense this, my mother tried leading me in a direction where the problem would surface. "Has something happened?"

"What do you mean?"

"I mean, has something happened between you and Laurel? Or did something happen to Laurel?"

"Her dog, Zelda, died."

"Oh no! I remember Pam talking about their dog when she'd go out to take care of Laurel's mother. I remember her vaguely. Pam said the dog would lay in bed with her, was really sweet. I'm guessing she had her for a long time?" she asked, laying her fork down on my plate.

"Laurel said they got her when she was a toddler."

"Oh, poor girl." Mom gave her head a sad shake. "And this happened the last time you saw her?"

"Yes."

"Wait a minute," Mom said, as though a lightbulb went off, and I was totally puzzled. "This happened the night you two went night fishing?"

"Yes."

"Did Zelda die while you two were out?"

"No."

"Oh, thank goodness." Mom let out a sigh of relief but then just as quickly scrunched her face up, mentally scrutinizing some fleeting thought. "When did you all find out, when did Zelda die?"

"Laurel missed a few phone calls." I tried not to blush, thinking about what Laurel and I were doing while her phone went ignored. Shame was followed by guilt. "But as soon as she realized she'd missed her dad's call, we packed up and I drove her back home."

"And then?"

"Her dad met us outside and told Laurel to hurry, that Zelda was going to go any minute."

"I'm glad she got the chance to say her goodbyes. What did you do after Zelda passed?" It almost looked like my mom was holding her breath in anticipation, and I couldn't understand why.

"Uh, I mean, I left."

Mom let out an exasperated sigh and crossed her arms, leaning to one side. "You left?"

"Well, yeah. I asked her if she wanted me to stay," I said half defensively, half ashamed because now, to hear what I'd done, or didn't do rather, made me feel embarrassed. "And she told me to go." I said the last part in a low, hushed tone, because saying it out loud made me believe that was what she actually wanted even less.

"Brayden Leon Anderson," Mom said. "Do you honestly think after losing a childhood pet, a pet she'd grown up with, that she really wanted to be alone? Have you called her? Gone to her house?"

"I was trying to give her space?" I shrugged.

"You didn't answer my questions."

"No. I texted her. And when she didn't answer, I texted Emily and found out she'd been staying there."

"Brayden, there is a time and place for giving space and being available. I don't want to butt into your relationship with Laurel, but be careful. I've dealt with a whole lotta grieving families in hospice, and I assure you, most of those folks treat their pets like a literal family member. This wasn't a goldfish that Laurel lost. This was the dog she grew up with, this was the dog that likely stayed by her side during the most difficult time in her life—when her mother died. This was the dog that also served to probably offset the loneliness Laurel's dad likely feels in having lost so greatly himself. This was the dog that, from what Pam tells me, was there in every way possible, every single day. And now she's dead too." Mom patted my arm, and before walking out of the room, she parted by saying, "Just be careful, Brayden. Be careful and be mindful. Also…" She paused, looking over her shoulder before vanishing into the living room. "Isn't prom in a few weeks? I haven't heard you mention anything about it."

I had so much to chew on.

Had I let Laurel down? Deep down in the pit of my stomach, I knew I had. Why would she want to be alone in her grief? I knew so little about it. Losing my grandparents was a bit of a foggy memory for me. I remember now, reflecting, being older, the signs of dementia that as a child I wasn't so sure about. I remember my parents' great sadness. Losing Mrs. McKenzie was terrible too, and I really hated it for Laurel because I knew it cut her far deeper. Did I not know how to process grief, hurt? I put my dirty plate in the sink and retreated to my bedroom to think about how to approach my next steps with Laurel.

****

I thought of a way to hopefully break the ice between Laurel and I and get back in her good graces. It was going to take some creative energy and a bunch of little kids, but I felt like I had the perfect plan. I got to the college where Laurel gave out piano lessons and hijacked the kids before she got there. I already had signs made and told them when they heard my drum roll, all they had to do was jump up and show Laurel their assigned signs.

No problem. What could go wrong?

****

I was nervous. I mean, I hadn't seen her in like four days. Emily assured me she was just taking it easy at her house, but my mom's words haunted me. I hoped this was good timing. Prom was literally in two weeks, and I hadn't asked her, really hadn't even thought about it until Mom brought it up. Maybe that I hadn't asked her already had her upset with me?

I walked to the back of the hallway where you'd normally walk in and planted myself behind the curtain. I could see the kids filing in, and in a few minutes, Laurel surfaced from behind them. They took their seats in the front row, and the one girl, Maddie, I think was her name, took her turn at the piano.

My hands were sweaty. My doubts and insecurities swam around like sharks smelling blood in my head. I could do this. I was supposed to do this. I grabbed my borrowed djembe, took a long and deep breath, and came out from behind the curtain.

I started beating the drum and instantly all eyes— Laurel's included—were on me. I searched for something in her gaze, anything that would inspire me to continue. That she didn't shut me down I guess was enough.

I winked at the kids, hoping they remembered their cue. They all shuffled to the stage with their cue cards, and lined up, revealing to Laurel why I was there.

In childlike words, sign number one read:

I've had to scale this back a bit…

Sign number two read:

…but you really are my forte…

Followed by all the musical notes and the last sign read:

…I hope this is clef-er enough for you … will you march to the beat of my drum and go to prom with me?

I couldn't see her face as she read these signs out loud, and my nerves were about as frayed as they could get, even more so than playing in the homecoming football game against our rivals.

Finally, after what felt like forever, Laurel turned around to face me.

Seeing her beautiful face never got old. Seeing the sadness in her gaze was new. She gave me a halfhearted smile, and my own heart dropped a little. Had I failed to recognize something? I felt sick, worried I'd been all wrong, that this was stupid, when she finally spoke up. Her voice soft and quiet, she said, "I'd love to go to prom with you."

And all my fears seemed to melt away, but I was missing something. Old doubts died only to be replaced with an army of new ones.

Laurel was sad. I could feel that across the auditorium.

How long would this last?

Chapter Twenty-Five

The May Queen

Brayden

It felt like Laurel and I had gotten back to some sense of normalcy, like how we were. I sensed a shadow of sadness that she seemed to be carrying around, but all I could hope for was in time, it would be gone.

I was excited and nervous about prom. I didn't know why. We'd been together all year, but somehow it was like that perpetual sense of doom was even more so tonight. Was it because this was the last school dance for her and me both?

I was unsure of so many things.

I pulled into her driveway, and it was odd to not have Zelda there to greet me. She really was gone. I knocked on the door and her dad answered.

"Hi," I said, giving a small wave to Scott as I waited on him to invite me in.

"Hey, come on in. She's almost ready. You can just wait here in the living room," he said, stepping out of the way so I could enter. "I'll be back. I need to go grab something from the studio."

I gave an awkward shrug of my shoulders and sat down on the couch. It was so quiet. I couldn't even hear Laurel from anywhere within the house. I stood up, stretched, and walked around looking at all their family photos.

Laurel looked like her mom.

An envelope sitting perched on one of their end tables caught my attention. But what really stood out were the bold red letters that read *Berklee*.

It was addressed to Laurel from the admissions department. Against everything my mother raised me to be, I picked it up, looked over my shoulder and around, and took the letter out.

My hands were shaking.

Dear Ms. Bennett,

Berklee is building the future of arts education— borderless in its availability and influence, pioneering in its embrace of innovation, and committed to empowering artists and creative leaders for lives of inspiration and impact.

We are a very competitive school, seeking excellence while representing over one-hundred and ten countries, home of three hundred thirty-three grammy alumni winners, and an endowment of over ninety million dollars. Our sacred halls have produced some of the finest musicians in the world.

We are very selective in choosing the recipients of our annual scholarships and after special consideration, we feel that you are deserving of the finalist category.

Congratulations for having made it this far. Our decision was based on originality, composition, and what we perceived to be raw, natural talent. You were selected as one of ten finalists from among one thousand talented entrants. As you know, only three students will be awarded the prestigious Berklee Endowment Scholarship for Excellence Award.

We look forward to your final audition and performance at the Robinson Grand on May 17th, promptly at six o'clock in the evening.

Warmest regards,

Sophia Markacelli, Procurement Specialist

I folded the letter, placed it back in its envelope, and set it down the way I found it.

I felt … sick.

I felt … betrayed.

I felt, I felt, I felt *anger* swell up inside of me.

Why hadn't she told me? When was she going to tell me? Ever? She was going to leave Czar, Buckhannon, Upshur County, West Virginia. She was going to Berklee, and she was going to leave … *me*.

I heard her doorknob turn, followed by the soft clicking of heels. As hurt as I was, and in a slight state of shock, she still took my breath away. She came to a stop in the living room, only a few feet from me. She wore a floor length red and black sequined dress with a low neckline and her hair swept up away from her face aside from the few strands that framed it. And she'd never looked more beautiful.

I gave her a forced smile as all my feelings were currently fighting each other in a deathmatch to see who'd emerge the victor. I'd never felt this way before.

"You look pretty," I said, extending the corsage out to her that I picked up earlier.

"Oh, um, thank you." She took the box. The smallest flash of confusion crossed her face as she fumbled with the box and then tried to put the corsage on.

I just stood there like an idiot.

"Here's yours," she said, grabbing a single red rose and clipping it to my jacket.

I looked down at her while she pinned me and up this close, I could see the rusty fleck in her iris, smell her light, clean perfume, and feel her little fingertips brush across my chest, and it almost made me forget what I'd just read.

Almost.

"Hey, let me grab a pic real quick before you two head out," Scott said as he came through the door.

I kept my gaze from Laurel's, afraid she could read my feelings. I slid my arm loosely around her waist and forced another smile.

"You two have fun, be safe, and be home by midnight," Scott said. All the while, he looked at me.

"Yes, sir."

I kept my gaze to the floor as I walked out. I hurried to the truck and opened the door, still avoiding her gaze. Once she had her skirt lifted up and she was seated, I shut the door. I was praying she'd put in a CD, anything to keep me from having to talk. I didn't quite trust myself yet.

As we pulled out, I felt her staring at me, and I had never been so uncomfortable. I tried to think quickly, come up with something to talk about before she caught on that I was upset.

"Chase and Emily are meeting us at Mama Mia's," I said, while keeping my gaze focused on the road. I felt her looking at me and it was unnerving. There definitely was so much hanging between us. "You feel like putting on one of those CDs you like?"

I could tell she sensed something was up. The air surrounding us was so thick. The tension was almost palpable. Thank God she popped one in. And it was like the others. I didn't know who the band was, but the only difference now was she wasn't singing along.

It felt like forever, but we finally reached Mama Mia's, and I was praying Chase and Emily were already there. The only thing I seemed to look forward to was being alone with Laurel. She was everywhere in my life. But now I was faced with the terror of being alone with her, with a truth I didn't want to confront. I didn't know how long I could go on like this.

I opened her door and helped her down, the feel of her hands in mine. I wanted to grab those fingers, hold onto her and believe the year we'd spent together wasn't her just killing time until she left for Berklee. The feeling that our relationship was nothing but a lie permeated my entire being. I was being consumed by a fire, the flames lashing upward, fanned by, by, by, what? Fear? Jealousy? Love?

As we walked into Mama Mia's it felt like there were a dozen sets of eyes on us. I scanned the area for Chase and Emily, and thank God, it only took a few moments for Emily to shoot up from their table and wave us down.

"Hey! Over here!"

I grabbed Laurel's hand, still averting my gaze from hers, and navigated my way through a maze of tables and booths toward the back of the restaurant.

"I ordered us some drinks, but we wanted to wait on you guys before we ordered food," Emily said, sitting back down beside Chase.

"They have some pretty sick pasta here," Chase said, skimming over the menu.

"You look gorgeous, Emily," I heard Laurel say. I flicked my gaze in their direction and then buried my own head in a menu. I needed to pull myself together, but these feelings were just brewing and festering, and I didn't know how to shove them down. They were so strong.

"Do you want to split a pizza?" Laurel asked. "Our usual?"

"Yeah, sure," I murmured. I briefly thought about that first time I brought her here so many months ago. Pineapple pizza. I'd never heard of let alone eaten pizza that way. That seemed a lifetime ago. Was it meaningless?

"Hey." Laurel leaned into me, whispering low. "Is everything okay?"

"Uh, yeah," I answered, shaking my head. "I was just thinking of stuff, that's all." I lied. Every word of it was a lie.

I didn't look her in the eye because she'd know. And I didn't know how I'd make it through the night like this, with the weight of the truth weighing down on all my better judgment.

I heard very little during our meal. I watched Emily and Chase laugh between each other, some inside joke, or maybe it was a full-fledged conversation, and I was so tuned out, I'd missed it. Laurel picked at her food, not saying much either. I was so worried she'd caught on to my mood, but I just didn't know how to stop it.

"Hey, you okay, man?" Chase piped up.

"Huh? Oh, yeah. Yeah, I'm cool." I gave a half-hearted smile. "You guys ready?" I just wanted to be anywhere but here. Gawd, it occurred to me that I was supposed to take Laurel over to my house for Mom to take pictures of us. I just couldn't.

"Yeah, let's blow this joint," Chase said, taking Emily's hand while throwing a fifty-dollar bill down on the table to cover the bill.

"I've got the tip," I said, remembering to act like a normal human.

Laurel grabbed my hand as we walked out of the restaurant. I both wanted to grab her up and pull her closer to me and also sling her hand away as though she'd burnt me. I felt like I couldn't breathe. When was she going to tell me? Did I not mean the same to her as she had me? Was I just filling in her time until she moved away to the big city where there were all kinds of like-minded, smart, musically gifted guys for her to pick and choose from?

God, this was driving me mad. Crazy. I couldn't focus on anything as I drove us to the college gym where prom was being held.

"What?" I heard myself answer. Laurel was talking to me in the truck as I drove, but I wasn't listening. I was past the point of hearing anything but my own thoughts.

"I was just asking what is wrong with you? Did something happen?" Laurel asked.

I caught the slightest look of worry and confusion flash across her face as she asked me this.

I pulled into the parking lot and found a spot relatively close to the entrance. There were all kinds of juniors and seniors filtering in through the double doors.

"Why would something be wrong? Don't you think if something was wrong, I'd tell you? You know, because honesty and all that means something."

"What do you mean? Where is this coming from?" Laurel asked, the hurt perhaps I was feeling was now surfacing in her own voice. Or maybe it was confusion. Whatever it was, it only made me madder. "You've had a problem since you picked me up. What is going on? What happened?"

I can look back now and see this for the missed opportunity it was, but I was so blinded by my own feelings of hurt and betrayal that I couldn't see the forest for the trees. "Doesn't matter what happened. You ready to go?" I didn't give her time to answer. I just jumped out of the truck, purposely slammed my door shut, and yanked hers open.

"Brayden," Laurel said, hurrying to get down. "Tell me what's going on?"

"No! How about *you* tell *me* what's going on?" I said, slamming her door shut, causing her to jump.

"I don't know what you mean," she said.

In the corner of my eye, I could see Emily and Chase pulling in a row over from us. I didn't care at this point. Nothing mattered. No one mattered. I was losing it.

"I saw your letter, you know, the one from

Berklee."

Her eyes widened in surprise, her mouth fell slightly agape, and it only angered me more and more, fuel on a fire that didn't need it to grow. What it needed was contained, but the fire had grown out of control. "Were you ever going to tell me?"

"You went through my mail?" she asked, the accusation crystal clear.

"Does it matter? Does it change anything?"

"Yes, how about trust?" She threw my words back at me.

"Oh, that's rich coming from you, Laurel. You actually want to play the trust card with me? I have been nothing but honest with you. What are we? What even am I to you? Some fucking country hillbilly with no hope of ever getting out of here, becoming something worthy of someone like you? Is that it? I'm just occupying your time until you move away to Boston where you can meet some rich dick who can take better care of you than me."

"Where is this coming from?" Laurel's voice was shaky. I'd hurt her and if I were being honest, I wanted her to hurt as bad as I was hurting. "I tried telling you about Berklee, about Boston."

"Oh really? When was that, Laurel? Was that when you told me you had an appointment when really you went for your first audition? Or was it all the time in between you receiving the letter inviting you for a second one that you tried telling me? Or was it at my parents' house the first time I took you there, when Caleb asked you and you gave him a half-assed answer? No, you didn't fucking try telling me. So, when exactly was that again?"

"I'm sorry, Brayden. I wanted to tell you. I just didn't know how. Because I was afraid of you acting like this. I was just waiting for the right time."

I could see Chase and Emily walking toward us. I didn't care. Didn't give two shits about who was around us at this point. My world was coming undone. Fuck everyone else.

"Oh, so you thought, when would be a good time? As your dad was driving you up to Boston?" I could feel the heat of anger race up my face, my cheeks burning. "Or were you going to let me do that, you know, one final fuck you."

"No—"

"Then when, Laurel?" I nearly screamed. "Were you going to break up with me?"

"Wait, what?" she asked, her face scrunched up in disbelief. "No. What are you talking about?"

"How are we supposed to work? Do you even care? Care that you're leaving me behind? Did I not mean anything to you?"

"Brayden, please, stop it," she said, tears forming in the corners of her eyes.

"No, Laurel. Because deep down, you know there's truth to what I'm saying. You want your cake and to eat it too. You knew I would stay here, take up the family business with my dad because I've been honest with you, from the fucking jump. You know I love you. Jesus, so help me, I do. And you were just stringing me along, not facing the problem of leaving me. Were you just going to peace out? Never saying anything?"

"No! I would never do that," she said defensively, tears rolling freely down her cheeks now.

"Hey, man. What's going on?" Chase asked from somewhere behind me.

I never even acknowledged him or the confusion in his voice.

"Then what do you want?" I said, through gritted teeth, my hands balled up in fists at my sides.

"I don't know," Laurel answered, softly.

"What. Do. You. Want?"

"Brayden—"

"No!" I cut her off. "Tell me! *What do you want*?"

"Hey," Emily cut in, walking up behind Laurel. "Guys, people are looking. I don't know what's going on, but maybe you two should chill for a sec."

I ignored her. The only thing I could seemingly focus on was all the rage, waves and waves of it, hitting me from all angles. "What do you want, Laurel? It's a simple question."

"Brayden," she said, shoving her hands through her hair, frustrated. "I don't know!" Her voice raised to match my own. "I don't know everything I want. Like right this very second, I just don't know. Stop trying to force me to make choices when I've not lived long enough to understand what both sides of those choices look like. What do I know? I know I have an opportunity to go to the college of my dreams, to learn from the very best. I know I want to be like my parents. I want to live. I want to be like my mom and experience more than Czar—"

I cut her off. "You want to be like your mom?" I asked, my voice was in a shredded state as I mocked her. I was coming undone, unhinged. Everything I loved before me was fleeting. Laurel was going to leave me. She was going to meet someone else. The thought of it drove me mad, crazy with jealousy. "Jesus Christ, Laurel. Why in the hell would you ever want to be like your mom? She committed suicide."

I heard the very audible intake of breath. From several people. They'd heard it all.

There are moments in life, moments so big, no amount of trying to redeem yourself will ever restore what was yours to lose in the first place. This was that moment, that moment that crossed the threshold of me having Laurel and me losing her. Her face twisted up in an almost feral state, half hate, half shock at words that cut her in the deepest of places, places I should've kept safe. She came at me like the wild animal my venomous words turned her into.

"You bastard!" she screamed, veins bulging out of her neck as she slapped me, the crack reverberating, the sound amplified by everyone's silence.

And I stood there, heart breaking, hating myself, taking slap after slap until broken by my words, Laurel's hits died down to nothing. All that was left were the sobs tearing from Laurel, sounds that were foreign, sounds that had been locked away long ago by a pain so deep they should've never been heard again. But I'd unlocked them, a vault of anguish and pain so deep the light of day should've never reached them.

Laurel was mine to lose. She was in my hands, her beautiful heart, and I let her slip right through my fingers.

"Come on, Laurel," Emily said, gathering her up and supporting her to walk. Emily looked over her shoulder at me in disgust. "You're a fucking dick, Brayden Anderson."

I looked around at the scene before me. Laurel was leaning onto Emily as she guided her to Chase's vehicle. I didn't try to stop her. It would have been too little, too late.

Chase walked after them but paused by me long enough to shake his head. He opened his mouth to speak, and I looked him square in the eye. But he closed his mouth and just shook his head again. Disbelief. Disappointment. All those things reflected in his gaze that I myself felt.

I looked out across the crowd. I recognized several people. All of them I went to school with. Had since I was a kid. No one said a word. Just looked at me as if seeing the monster I was. I waited for the rotten cabbage to be thrown. But that never happened. Just continued looks of disbelief that I'd stooped so low until finally, having enough of the spectacle I'd created, they all filed into the gym until I was left all alone.

With no company but my anguish and self-loathing.

I could never take back what I said. Never make right the colossal wrong I'd created against the one I loved most.

What had I done?

Chapter Twenty-Six

I'll Remember You

Laurel

Having a haptic memory was a blessing when, say, you wanted to recall how to play an instrument you rarely played. Haptic memory came in pretty handy then. When trying to let the pain dull from losing your mother to suicide? Haptic memory was a curse. It was my absolute worst enemy because there was nothing I could do to forget.

Brayden coming into my life when he did, I had always thought was a blessing, my good fortune. He always felt … *right*. Never in a million years would I have thought he'd hurt me in the worst way. He'd had me relive the worst day of my life, a memory that surfaced every single day but was made more bearable because of him, because I thought he truly loved me.

I was so numb after pummeling him, I barely remember Emily helping me to Chase's car. I sat down in the back seat, Chase and Emily conversing between themselves in hushed tones I didn't care to hear anyhow, when the pain of the past exploded in my mind as I closed my eyes.

I was back there, four years ago.

****

Marie

"Are you sure?" Scott asked Marie, his face nothing but conflicted lines of turmoil.

"Of course I'm sure. I feel great, and besides, Pam will be here in like thirty minutes. Go! Shoo!" Marie waved at her husband, Scott, and their only child, Laurel.

She watched as they both went toward the door.

"Hey!" Marie yelled. "I better get a hug and a kiss, you two!"

Laurel ran over to where her mom was sitting and bent down to hug her.

Marie squeezed her a little extra tight and kissed her cheek. She held her there and whispered, "Your mama loves you so."

"I love you too, Mom." Laurel answered her with a smile.

"You get some strawberry ice cream for me."

"I will," Laurel said, stepping aside so Scott could kiss his wife goodbye.

"Take your time, Scott. Enjoy some ice cream with the kiddo. It's been a long winter. How nice to finally have a warm day, sunshine, and ice cream. Ah." Marie sighed dreamily while smiling up at her husband.

"Hey! I'm not a kid!" Laurel said, with an accusatorial smile.

"My child you'll always be, missy," Marie said. "Remember that."

"Love you, my Marie," Scott said as he bent down and kissed his wife.

"You're the apple of my eye, love you till the day I die," Marie said in a lowered voice she only meant for Scott to hear. "Now you can go."

Marie sat propped up in her recliner. Today was a good day. She wasn't in any pain. Her mind was clear. The cancer had seemed to choke out every aspect of her life, like her distinction between reality and delusion thanks to it chipping away at her nervous system.

But today was like no other day. She was clear-minded, pain free, it was sunny, and it was also her time. Marie had been given six months to a year to live thanks to the invasive metastatic brain cancer she'd been diagnosed with. What started as mild headaches had progressed into a death sentence. There were days she had seizures, some days she vomited nonstop, other days she couldn't get out of bed. And then her personal favorite, the hallucinations the brain cancer produced made her live at times in a distorted reality that was utterly terrifying.

The worry she saw on her husband and their fourteen-year-old daughter was almost too much to bear. They were so brave, but sometimes when they thought she was sleeping, she could hear her daughter cry and her husband trying comfort her, telling her to be strong, that they both had to be strong for Mom.

Now today was her turn to be strong for the loves of her life, a husband she never knew how she was so lucky to land, the beautiful soul he was, and the beautiful soul they'd created—their darling, darling daughter, Laurel.

She removed the afghan covering her and stood on slightly shaky legs. She took a deep breath and walked slowly toward the medicine cabinet. "Zelda." She leaned down to scratch her on the head. "How glad I am that you are here with me. Stay with me until the end and then it's up to you to take care of Scott and Laurel. They are going to need all your love, sweet girl."

Zelda gave a little whine, as though she suspected something out of the ordinary was occurring. Marie walked over and opened the cabinet containing all of her hospice meds—Haldol, Zofran, Tylenol suppositories, Ativan, and the one she was looking for specifically— morphine.

Marie felt good enough to walk outside, but she knew she didn't have much time. She wanted one last look at the beautiful mountain home her husband secured for them with this art. Scott was a dreamer, always had been, but he showed her that sometimes dreams do come true.

He'd made all of hers a reality. Her heart ached at the thought of the pain that was to come for those she loved more than the moon. She took one sweeping last glance and walked back in and perched herself up in her recliner.

She pulled out her cell phone and dialed her nurse, Pam. Service wasn't always the best, but after a few rings, Pam answered.

"Marie? Is everything okay?"

"I need you to come here in about fifteen minutes. Thank you, Pam, truly, for everything you've ever done. You've been an angel, don't ever forget that."

"Marie—" Pam started, the worry clear in her voice, but Marie hung up, and while she still had courage, she downed the entire bottle of liquid morphine. She knew she only had a few minutes before succumbing to a place she'd never come back from.

She pulled out the letters she'd prepared for Scott and Laurel.

"Stay with me, girl," Marie whispered to Zelda, stroking her between the ears like she liked. She read her letter to Scott first.

A million lifetimes would never be enough with you, Scott. You've made my life a happy one with your heart, with your tender soul, with your beautiful dreamer's mind. Forgive me, my darling. I wanted you forever. This isn't our first love story, and it won't be our last. We will always find each other. In every lifetime. That is my promise to you. And now I leave you with the best part of me—our little girl, our beautiful, beautiful Laurel. She'll need you, so many times she will need you. I'll be seeing you, Scott. You're the apple of my eye. I'll love you till the day I die. And then some. ~ Your Marie

And then she read her note to her daughter.

I don't expect you to understand. I know you are

going to hurt for a long, long time. All I can do is apologize for that and wish I could somehow take on that hurt for you. I want you to remember your mama as I was—healthy and whole. I'm sorry the universe is robbing you. It's important that you know you were always loved. You were planned. And the happiest day of my life was December sixteenth, at eight o'clock in the morning, fourteen years ago. I'll always remember the feel of your little body being laid into my arms, and how your cheeks actually bounced. I've never loved anyone more than you. Nor have I been prouder. My girl, I pray all your childhood dreams come true—that you'll meet someone like your father who you love, and they love you in return, that you'll be happy and healthy, and that you'll never forget how much your mama loved you. You are my greatest gift to the world. Remember, there are only two kinds of people in this world—good people and bad people, no more, no less. Always give away your excess—someone needs it. Always dream and shoot for those dreams. Listen to your dad, he loves you so. You are exactly what I wished for in a child—you're kind, beautiful, and have a gentle soul and heart. As I close my eyes, I can hear you play and sing and know those are my greatest joys. Laurel, take care of your father. He will need you. Your mama loves you. Forever.

A tear rolled down her cheek as she folded up the letter and placed it with the other one on her stand. She kept her hand on Zelda, her breaths becoming shallower. She felt the weight of life being slowly lifted, as though she herself could float, and before losing all consciousness, she knew it was the effects of the morphine. She knew she only had a few minutes left in this world before she was no longer part of it.

God in heaven how she'd miss her husband and daughter. She didn't want to leave them. She both cursed *her cancer for her short life but also thanked God for giving her family to her for the time she had them.*

She hated to put the burden of finding her lifeless body on her nurse, Pam. But sometimes the body failed you in epic ways, and it was important to her to have Scott and Laurel remember her as she was instead of some emaciated version of what she'd once been. And the hardship would have to fall on someone more seasoned than her tenderhearted family.

There were some things in life a person could never unsee and they'd haunt them forever. It was important to Marie, it was the last thing she could do for her family, to ensure they remembered her with all her functions. Pam would make sure she was presentable.

"Zelda..." Marie whispered before the final image of Scott and Laurel flashed before her eyes, eyes that were closing forever.

How she loved them.

****

Laurel

Riding in the backseat of Chase's car, mascara running down my face, all I could think of was Pam meeting my dad and I outside on the porch. I could see her face like it was yesterday, the burden of having to tell us my mom died written all over her. Oddly, I could still hear myself scream and scream and scream, a nightmare I never thought I'd wake from.

My mama was beautiful. She had long blonde hair, green eyes, a gentle voice, and she encouraged me in everything I ever did. I was homeschooled until she died. And then I wanted to go to school so I could try to occupy my mind with things other than looking at the recliner she died in, day in and day out. I clung onto that afghan as though the woman I loved were still wrapped up in it.

All the whispers behind my back came flooding back. When I enrolled in school and started, rumors swirled around that child protective services forced my dad to put me in school. Or my personal favorite—that my mother was a junkie, a drug addict. It was hurtful hearing jerk kids desecrate my happy childhood and chalk up my attendance to being enforced because I had some kind of abusive father, when in reality, I had the best father in the world. I also had the best mother, but she died—killed herself to preserve a memory she hoped my father would have of her versus the memory she was scared her cancer would force us to live with.

My heart would surely burst. This pain was unbearable.

I dared to dream like my mother's letter instructed me to.

I dared to love like she encouraged me to.

I dared, I dared, I dared, and now all I was left with was a shattered dreamer's heart. I would never get over this betrayal.

Never.

SASHA HIBBS

Chapter Twenty-Eight

The Murder of a Songbird

Brayden

I was an idiot, the biggest fool. So stupid. I didn't know how long I stood in the college parking lot simply looking into thin air as though Laurel would come back to me, as though I was waiting for some kind of time traveling device to materialize from thin air, allowing me to go back and fix my stupid, stupid mistake.

All of my mistakes.

"Stupid! Stupid! Stupid" I screamed, hitting myself in the face.

There were so many people I knew that stared at me, gawking at the whole damn mess I'd created. Coach Westfall just walked by. Never had I seen such an unimpressed look on his face, not even when we lost our biggest football game of the season. Kids I'd gone to school with my entire life, teachers ... this was a small town. Everyone knew everyone. Except Laurel. She'd been homeschooled most of her life and when she finally did enroll in Buckhannon Upshur, she'd kept her personal life to herself, even allowing rumors to fly. Because that's how confident she was. People could talk about her all day and night, and regardless of how untrue, she just kept being herself. She didn't care what people had to say. She knew the truth.

But I knew Laurel. I knew of the biggest skeleton in her closet—her mother's suicide. And not that she should ever be ashamed of that. But it should've been protected. And what did I do? Drug that skeleton right out of the vault and paraded it around for the whole damn town to see.

I had to get out of here. I jumped up in the truck

and just drove and drove and drove until finally I found myself at Stonecoal Lake, where I'd taken Laurel before. I never played CDs. That's what she did. I glanced down and saw Creedence Clearwater Revival. I could almost picture her sitting beside me on a sunny day, looking out her window and humming along to whatever tune, because she knew them all. And my chest ached.

With shaky hands, I opened the case and popped in the CD. As soon as the first notes hit my ears, I closed my eyes and was surrounded by Laurel. Everything Laurel. I felt her absence. I got out of the truck and walked to where we were that night. I looked down and envisioned her there, wearing her flannel, looking at me with honesty and love, and I burned with shame.

I wanted to crawl out of my skin. I shoved my hands through my hair. I looked up into the sky and just screamed.

I ran back to the truck, ejected the CD, and smashed it in a million pieces. I crushed all of them. And then fell to my knees. I felt hot tears burn in the corners of my eyes and I did nothing to stop them from falling down. I felt helpless. I felt stupid. I felt miserable and ashamed.

I sat there hunched over on my knees for what felt like forever before I gathered the strength to stand and somehow find myself back into my truck. I opened my phone.

Nothing.

No messages.

No phone calls.

No texts.

Just my screensaver—a picture of us together—staring back at me.

I opened up Instagram. I couldn't find her.

I opened up Snapchat. Nothing.

I pulled up her number.

The cold realization that I'd been blocked hit me. I knew I deserved it. But it stung. How could I ever face her? How could I ever apologize enough for the vicious thing I'd said? I pulled up old videos I had of her singing. Laurel was a beautiful songbird, and I'd committed the greatest sin against her.

My heart constricted, squeezed in on itself so tight, I thought it would surely burst. I prayed for the relief of it. But relief never came. No rest for the wicked as the saying goes. I remembered the night I recorded her. She was playing at open mic. I could see her slender fingers glide across the piano keys, and then onto the guitar, her voice reaching up into the heavens. No one was like Laurel. She was so special. And she was mine. And I lost her.

I couldn't bear this. I just couldn't. I had to make it right. I put the truck in drive and desperation seemed to make me fly to Laurel's house. I pulled in, left the truck running, and ran up, pounding on the door.

Scott answered, a look on his face that conveyed he knew something was up. I didn't know how much though. And honestly, if he punched me, I'd deserve it.

"Is Laurel here? Can I please speak with her?" I was so desperate. I would make her understand I didn't mean any of what I'd said. We could go back to how we were. We'd figure out Berklee. I could see that now. Not having her was the biggest obstacle. So, what if it was a long-distance relationship? The thought of not having her in my life at all was too great and terrible to even think about.

"Yes, she is here, and no, you can't speak with her," he said firmly, unmoved by the panic on my face I took no trouble to hide.

"Please, I'm begging you," I said, the alarm in my

voice clear at the possibility of never seeing her again. This couldn't be happening. God, what I'd do to go back.

"I said, no. No means no. If she wants to see you, she'll reach out to you."

"Please, I'm so sorry. I just need to tell her."

"We can at least agree on that," Scott said, his face curled up in disgust. "You *are* sorry."

I could see the resolve on his face. There was no way he was letting me past him to see his daughter. "Please tell her I'm sorry. I'm so sorry."

He remained silent, watching me until I was out of sight. I ran over to her window and screamed at the top of my lungs. "I'm sorry, Laurel. Jesus. I'm so fucking sorry."

I was met with silence.

****

"Brayden, what's happened?" my mom said.

Both my parents came outside when I pulled in. I imagine I was quite the sight—disheveled, coming unglued. I had dried blood on my knuckles from where I'd punched something—was it my truck door? I didn't know. My feelings seemed to swing between desperation to violence.

"Are you hurt? Where's Laurel?" Dad asked, his voice a little more composed than Mom's.

I looked back and forth between them. I didn't trouble myself to downplay anything I'd done. I'd murdered my songbird, silencing her against me forever.

"I hurt Laurel."

"What do you mean?" Dad asked. "Brayden?"

I could see the fear on both my parents' faces. I didn't know what they thought I was capable of, but this was my lowest moment. I couldn't get within reach of Laurel, but I could lay my sins out before my parents.

"I took her trust in me and killed it out of

jealousy."

"What do you mean, Brayden?" Mom gently asked. She inched closer to me. I couldn't tell if she was afraid of me, or for me. Maybe both.

I'd never felt smaller, weaker, or more ashamed of myself as I told both my parents, looking them in the eyes, what I'd done to Laurel.

"Son," my dad said in a voice almost too low to hear. "I'm not sure what to say. You were raised better than that."

"I know. You're right." It was all my lame ass could come up with.

"Brayden, you need to give her some space. You both need space," Mom said, gently laying her hand on my shoulder. I knew she meant to comfort me, that was in her nature, but I didn't deserve it.

The only thing I deserved was to feel this way.

"Sometimes we say things we don't mean. And, unfortunately, those things we don't mean, we can't take back. All you can do now is show her you are sorry versus telling her," Dad added. There was disappointment in his eyes but no judgment. They both loved me and somehow that made me feel worse. It was like I somehow needed to start over, find a way to be worthy of love.

How would I show her? How could I ever begin to show her how sorry I was? How would I ever bear this?

SASHA HIBBS

Chapter Twenty-Nine

Emotional Debris

Laurel

I had a plan. I was going to put everything I had and then some into auditioning and hopefully landing a scholarship to Berklee. I asked myself so many times growing up why I'd been given a haptic memory, and not even the short version which is usually what haptic people dealt with.

Nope. Not me. I had long term. So, I never forgot a thing. Not. One. Damn. Thing.

What didn't I plan for?

Brayden.

I'd never told him about my mom's suicide or the circumstances surrounding it. I didn't want her suicide to ever define her, for that to be what people remembered about her. When people talked about my mom, I wanted them to talk about what a wonderful human being she was. How magical and creative, a true free spirit. Not that she'd killed herself.

I sat across from my therapist, Melissa, who I hadn't seen in a long, long time. Dad thought it would be good for me to see her. I knew he was only worried about me, but it was hard to relive hell over and over again. I guess talking to someone with no skin in the game helped, but I was resentful to even be in this situation to begin with.

"It's been a while, Laurel. Would you like to tell me what's been going on? What is it that brings you here today?" she asked, crossing her legs while leaning back in her seat. "Don't misunderstand, I'm happy to see you, but generally people don't see me because they are popping in to tell me how great they are. In my line of work, no news is good news."

I took a deep breath. "I've been seeing this boy."

"Okay."

"Like pretty much all year. Brayden is his name."

"I see," she said. "Tell me about Brayden."

I could feel that old familiar knot welling up in my throat. I took a sip of water and leaned back in my chair. "We met right before summer ended, at the beginning pretty much of the school year. He's a football player—"

"A football player?" she asked, cutting me off, her eyebrows arched in what appeared to be surprise.

"Yeah, I know. Surprising, isn't it?"

"They say opposites attract," she commented. "Go on."

"Right, well we started dating, and I thought he was amazing. He'd come to open mic, watch me perform. He'd come with me to where I give music lessons. And he was so good with the kids. He was so kind. I spent Christmas with his family. His parents are great. He was so supportive." I could feel myself losing the battle as I fought back tears. I'd already cried so much I couldn't imagine crying anymore. I was so tired of crying.

I'd worked with Melissa long enough to know she could sense the internal struggle. Giving me a few moments to compose myself, she asked a few questions. "You're talking about this boy in past tense. I'm assuming you two broke things off?"

I nodded.

"Okay. So, let's refresh and make sure I have it all correct. You met Brayden at the beginning of the school year. He's kind, supportive, you like his parents. Am I correct so far?"

I shook my head yes.

"So, there are large missing parts of this story.

How did you two break things off? Do you want to tell me about that?"

I really didn't, but I had to.

"Brayden knew my mom died, but I never told him she killed herself. He found out I was a step closer to getting into Berklee, and on prom night he freaked out on me over it and then…" I swallowed hard. This part hurt me so bad I had no words. "We fought over it. I felt pressured about our relationship, like how it was going to work, and he kept pushing me for an answer. I told him I didn't know, that I didn't have the answers, and that—" I felt the tears welling up again in my eyes. "I wanted to live, and be carefree like my mom, and then he screamed at me." I started crying. The ache in my chest was too much to bear.

"Screamed? What did he say?" Melissa asked, trying to gently guide me.

"He screamed at me, asking me why I would ever want to be like my mom because in the end she killed herself."

There was no audible shock, no gasp of disbelief from Melissa. "I'm sorry you went through that." She scooted the box of tissues over toward me. "Laurel, I've seen you on and off since your mother died. And this was the longest stretch of time I've not seen you. I feel like there's still some missing pieces of this story. Let me ask you questions and see if I can get more of a picture and feel for what's been going on."

"Okay," I said.

"I know you had a high regard for Mrs. McKenzie, and I read where she passed away sometime during the winter. I'm sure that was hard for you. You and Brayden were together during this time, correct?"

"Yes."

"Was he supportive? Did he understand how

deeply you felt for Mrs. McKenize?"

"I think so."

"Hmm. It's also my understanding from your dad that your family pet, Zelda, has recently died."

"We got her when I was four. She was like my sister," I answered, crying freely. I wasn't sure how much I could handle being laid out all at one time.

"Was Brayden there, did he try to help you grieve these losses?"

I thought about it before answering too quickly. "I think maybe he tried to be."

"Do you know if Brayden has ever lost anyone close to him?"

"He told me his grandparents died when he was young."

"I see, I see," she said thoughtfully. "Laurel, we all experience grief differently. Wouldn't you agree with that?"

"Yes."

"Well, grief hits us differently at various ages, my point being Brayden, while I wouldn't want to diminish the loss of his grandparents, he might have been too young to feel the full impact of such a loss. Does that make sense to you?"

I had never given it any real consideration before. "Yes, I suppose so."

"My point is, you say Brayden was supportive of all your creative endeavors minus you going to Berklee, and in the same breath I'm hearing, or at least getting the feeling he kind of left you hanging when you lost some of those closest to you. I think it's possible Brayden doesn't fully understand grief, how to process it, or how to be there for someone who is going through it or had past trauma."

I considered her words and tried to see it from her

perspective. It was hard to see anything through the storm clouds.

"And let me ask you, why was Brayden surprised, or maybe angry is the better word to use to describe his feelings, about you trying to get into Berklee?"

"When he and I first started dating, I mentioned in passing that I had thought about going to Berklee." I paused for a moment, thinking back to all those months ago. "No, that's not right. I didn't mention Berklee, exactly. But his brother asked me about getting into a program like Julliard."

"But did you explore with him what that really meant? Did he have a firm understanding? Why was he then surprised by your second audition? Did he know about the first one?" she asked, and there was no judgment in her voice. I could tell she truly was collecting facts to try and analyze them.

"No. I hid it from him."

"Why?"

"I was afraid he wouldn't accept it and wouldn't support my decision to go."

"I think I see now," she said, tapping a finger against her chin. "Brayden saying what he did about your mom was uncalled for. No amount of misunderstanding or desperation on his part would ever make that behavior acceptable. But I want you to consider a few things."

"Desperation?" I asked, puzzled.

"Yes. After stitching this together, someone as supportive of you as what you describe Brayden to be wouldn't just suddenly be unsupportive. His desperation was born out of fear of losing you altogether. Desperation will make people do foolish things, say malicious things. I want you to consider that maybe you not being one hundred percent honest with this boy triggered a poor reaction on his part. Not making excuses but trying to get you to understand logic and human nature. Also, it's important to be honest with yourself. You kept the try-outs or auditions quiet and to yourself because deep down you knew or expected a poor reaction from Brayden, so rather than deal with it, he found out the wrong way about you going rather than hearing it from your lips. It's important because I imagine he feels your time together was perhaps one-sided and diminishes his belief that you ever cared for him if you were willing to keep such a huge part of your future secret from him knowing it would have a huge impact on his future as well, at least this is if you two were going to try and maintain the relationship."

"It really doesn't matter now," I said, feeling so defeated.

"What makes you say that?"

"I didn't go to my audition."

"Was that the only one you could go to?"

"Yes."

She looked at me for what felt forever before speaking. "As your therapist I'd be remiss not to advise you to be aware of self-loathing behavior. You deserved that audition. As another human being going through the world at the same time as you, who cares about you, I'm sorry to hear you missed that. You hurting yourself this way will not take back the things Brayden said to you, it won't reverse anything, and it certainly wouldn't make your mother happy."

I opened my mouth to speak, but words wouldn't come out.

"I think you need to take some time and sort through all these feelings. Brayden, it sounds like, was your first love and first loves are intense. You're a musical savant, Laurel. While I'm sad to hear about your audition, nothing is final but death, and even in death we leave those closest to us behind to remember us and keep us alive in that way. Music will always be part of your life. You will find your way back to where you were meant to be in that regard. Time has a way of making things look clearer."

SASHA HIBBS

Chapter Thirty

Graduation

Brayden

It had been two weeks and nothing. Not one word. Not one text. Nothing. Laurel's dad made it perfectly clear not to come back over, and I knew I'd pressed my luck going there the first night. I didn't know how to reach her. I didn't know how, like my dad said, to show her I was sorry. She'd missed school since prom night. Emily dodged my every attempt to communicate through her, and even Chase, my friend since kindergarten, refused to get involved.

My last hope was that Laurel would show up for graduation. Surely, she would. After all, how many times did you get to graduate from high school? I ran through my head a million times what I'd say to Laurel as soon as I had the opportunity to see her. I was such an idiot. I was so selfish. So blind.

My entire graduating class shuffled into the gymnasium. We'd practiced having it outside, but a downpour came. My gaze went back and forth between all the exits and entrances, praying she was running behind. Everyone was taking their places and nothing. No Laurel. No Scott. No one. I ran quickly over to Emily.

I was met with a look of complete disgust.

I hunched down beside her, almost rooting McKayla Smith out of her seat. "Please, Emily. I'm begging you. Where is she?"

"You're a dick, you know that, right?"

"Yes. I do. But please tell me she's coming here tonight." The principal took the stage, walking up to the microphone, and the crowd grew silent. I whispered so only Emily could hear me. I didn't give two shits about what the principal had to say.

"No, she is not, asshole. In fact, that audition that had you so pissed off, well, she didn't go to that either."

"What do you mean? She missed it?" I asked in disbelief. I was sick. This couldn't be happening.

"Yeah, she did. Now please get away from me. You're not getting anything else out of me. You've done enough damage."

"Please tell her I'm sorry." I felt so desperate to reach her on some level.

"You're kidding, right? After bringing up her mom's suicide the way you did, you think I'd help you?" Emily shook her head in disgust. "You're on your own."

I stood up, not caring that there were hundreds of eyes on me as I shuffled back to my assigned seat. I wasn't going to get anywhere with Emily. And I honestly didn't blame her. I blamed myself. My head was swimming. I couldn't believe what Emily just told me about Laurel missing the opportunity of a lifetime. And I hated myself even more.

At some point, the principal called my name and it took the kid sitting next to me elbowing me in the side to get my attention. Everything felt mechanical now. I managed to walk up to the stage, accept my diploma, and shuffle back to my seat. I couldn't focus on anything. The guilt was almost too much to bear. I thought back to that night so long ago when I was walking up Main Street and her voice trailed around the corner as though taking literal shape, taunting me to follow it. I'd never heard anything or anyone sound so soulful, so haunting, so otherworldly. And then I got to know her and discovered that *she* was otherworldly. And I'd crushed her, ruined her dreams, ones that she was destined to live out.

I had to make this wrong right, or I'd never be able to live with myself. Not having Laurel was a pain I had to shove way down deep, but the thought of not having her in my life while simultaneously killing her dreams—I couldn't and wouldn't live with that.

I knew my parents and brother were out in the crowd somewhere. I didn't want to deprive them of celebrating and lord knows, I loved them. But I'd robbed another. The one I loved. And it was hard to put on a face, wear a mask as though nothing was wrong when it felt like the ground under my feet was caving while the sky was falling in on me.

After what felt like a lifetime of awards, and scholarship announcements—which felt like salt in the wound at this point—graduation came to an end. My parents and brother were quick to sort me out.

"You did it, son! We are all so proud of you," Dad said, my brother beside him smiling while slapping me on the back. My mother smiled at me, but I felt like out of the entire family, she and I were connected on another level. She knew what was in my heart, how I was hurting. She gave me a sad smile, and I understood it for what it was—happiness that I'd graduated, but sadness because she knew my heart was broken.

We had dinner out and I heard little. Saw little. Cared even less.

"Thanks, you guys," I said, after finishing off what I knew on a different day, would've been the best meal ever.

I knew what I had to do and prayed in the end it mattered, made a difference for the one I loved most.

****

I'd only ever driven to Charleston, West Virginia, or even Morgantown a time or two. And that was about as city as it got for me. I wasn't used to one lane roads, and DO NOT ENTER streets, one-way this and one-way that, and lights and traffic hell, and it was all a bit terrifying, but for Laurel I'd do anything.

I'd never dreamt of going to Boston a day in my life, but then again, I never thought I'd meet and lose someone as beautiful as Laurel, someone whose soul shined like hers did. It killed me with shame to think I dimmed such a glowing light. It was hell finding the Genko Uchida Center even with the 921 Boylston Street address plugged into my Google Maps, but I'd try to navigate my way through hell for Laurel.

I'd driven for hours, and as I pulled up to what looked like an old grand, and I mean *grand*, theater, I finally found a place to park. My truck looked out of place. I didn't care. After paying for a parking pass, I jogged around the corner and up a set of large, concrete steps. I was looking for admissions. I walked in hesitantly, hoping I didn't stick out like a sore thumb.

The smell of instruments hit me. A certain kind of wood coupled with the cleaner used to polish them infiltrated my every sense. And it reminded me of her, of going with her while she taught a bunch of kids to play the piano. She belonged in these halls.

After roaming around several corridors, I finally found a set of offices labeled *Admissions*. I walked in and found myself looking down at a middle-aged lady who in turn was looking down her nose at me through huge, black thick-framed glasses.

"Can I help you?"

"Yes, please. I need to speak to Sophia Markacelli," I said, trying to appear relaxed, like I somehow belonged here.

"Do you have an appointment?" she asked, her Boston accent thick and intimidating.

My heart sank, but I took courage. "No, ma'am."

"Well, you have to have an appointment," she said, turning her attention back to her computer as though

I wasn't even there.

"Excuse me, ma'am," I said, remaining calm. "But it's important. I really need to speak to her."

"What is your name?"

"Brayden Anderson."

She furiously punched on her keyboard with angry fingertips and then gave me a glare. "See here," she began, pointing at her screen. "It appears there is no Brayden Anderson scheduled to see Ms. Markacelli. You are welcome to leave your information, and I will pass it along when I see her."

"I drove ten hours to get here. I'm begging you, it's important." I would *not* leave here until I fixed what I'd broken.

"Do I need to call security, young man?"

"No, you need to call Ms. Markacelli. I know she's here. I called earlier before driving ten hours to see her."

I watched her pick up the phone and talk under her breath, almost whispering. I knew she wasn't calling her. I looked around frantically. I had no idea what this lady looked like, but I was running out of time before I got escorted out of the building, or worse, had the cops called on me. There were a series of offices behind the secretary, and I looked for any clues that would give away who Ms. Markacelli was.

Bingo!

I saw a golden plaque with her name on it, and I shot behind the counter without another thought.

"Excuse me! You *cannot* come back here! You have to have an appointment!" she screamed. I heard her from somewhere behind me frantically calling security, and I knew my time was even more limited.

I opened the glass door to see a very unimpressed looking woman staring back at me as though nothing annoyed her more than my presence. I had to move a mountain with what felt like a plastic sand shovel, and I only had seconds to do it.

"Ms. Markacelli, you don't know me, but you might be familiar with the name Laurel Bennett." I paused only a moment to see if there were any signs of recognition. "She missed her audition three weeks ago. From West Virginia."

She crossed her arms and leaned up. "Oh, yes. I remember her. What a pity."

"Please, I'm begging you. Give her a second chance."

"Do you think the world is run off of second chances? Our institution of higher learning isn't in a shortage of talented people seeking free tuition to one of the most prestigious schools in the United States. Ms. Bennett had an opportunity. Matter of fact, she had a one in a thousand opportunity. And she chose not to accept what was likely hers for the taking had she only cared to show up."

"I understand, but—"

She cut me off angrily. "There are no buts. We don't nurse the disappointed hopes of hundreds of other kids who didn't get the chance Ms. Bennett did. And we most certainly do not entertain another opportunity after being stood up. Do you realize I, myself, personally drove to oversee Ms. Bennett's audition? I had such high hopes."

"It's my fault. I'm begging you. I'll do whatever it takes. I was her boyfriend, she trusted me, and I did something unforgivable to her," I said in a rush, my stomach in knots as I heard the shuffle of feet behind me, the door opening. It felt like the sand in my hourglass was nearly run out.

"Please escort this young man outside, and if he

doesn't leave once out of our building, call the police," she said in a flat, unmoved tone.

"She worked hard for this. You've heard her. Laurel was born, was *made* for music. The world of music would be a sadder place without her in it."

She nodded to the security guards, signaling them to physically escort me out of her office. My moment was fleeting, slipping through my hands just like Laurel slipped through my fingers. I couldn't allow this to be final no more than I could stop breathing.

They placed their hands on me, giving me a stern redirection to leave. I had one card left I could play. I'd saved up all my chips, hoping it wouldn't come to this. But now it was time to cash them in.

"Laurel has a haptic memory. A long term one at that!" I screamed through the door, craning my neck around the security guards, ensuring she could hear me.

"Wait! Stop!" I heard her say, and as the guards halted and eased up slightly on their grasp of me.

I straightened myself out and turned back around in her direction.

She stood up from her desk. I could see her ears almost perk up like a dog's would. "Let him go, please."

This was the break I'd been praying for. I had to get this right. I knew Laurel wanted in on her talents and skill alone—she was everything that was good and innocent in that way—but desperation would make you do things you normally wouldn't. I didn't care what I had to do or say to get a few minutes of this lady's undivided attention.

Laurel deserved no less.

"Pray, continue, uh, Mr...." She didn't know my name.

"Anderson. But please. I go by Brayden and that

really isn't important."

"You were saying?" She motioned for me to take a seat across from her on the other side of her desk.

I lowered myself down into the chair. I quickly pulled out my phone that I'd already had set to play the song that started it all. I knew how enchanted I was. I couldn't imagine being more swept off my feet than hearing the raw voice with nothing but a small ukulele to accompany it. Her voice was the truth. That she could play any instrument in her hand was just icing on the cake.

I hit play and launched into what I'd hope would be a persuasive argument. So much—Laurel's entire future—rode on me getting this right. My hands were sweaty, and my stomach was in knots knowing all the miles of wrong I had to make right in such a short time.

"Laurel was born to become something greater, something shared, part of something more than just herself, more than a small town. We all have a haptic memory to a degree. But it doesn't last. That Laurel's does should speak to the truth of the fact that she was born to become a star. And she shines so bright," I said, leaning forward in my chair. "For more reasons than her ability to play and recall every piece of musical equipment put in her hands. Because she's a good human being, and she is capable of taking that greatness and goodness inside of her and letting you and the rest of the world hear what I can only conclude God gifted her with." I paused, allowing the haunting melody and even more haunting voice of Laurel to seep in around our conversation as she sang and played to Hank Williams in a recording of, *I'm So Lonesome I Could Cry*.

I wasn't sure if she was moved by my speech as she kept a pretty straight face, but as I was getting ready to pick up where I'd left off, she stopped me. "Well,

Brayden, that's quite the soliloquy. And while I'm impressed with Laurel, which is why she was chosen as a finalist to begin with, we have never made an exception in my twenty-two years here for anyone that has missed their second audition. Tell me why I should make an exception in her case?"

And here's where it was time to pay for my sins. I just hoped it would be enough to buy Laurel's way in. I had to lay my confession out for her to do with what she would. I took a deep breath and without flinching, held her gaze the entire time I gave her my account of how I'd taken Laurel's most painful secret and used it against her out of petty jealousy, out of fear she'd leave me behind and go on to do greater things without me.

"I betrayed her. I knew what would cripple her, and I destroyed her with something I should've protected," I said, still burning with the shame I felt for what I'd done to the beautiful soul that Laurel was.

"I see," she said while lightly tapping her nails on her wooden desk. "I imagine it took a great deal of courage to come up here and face what you'd done in an attempt to remedy the situation."

"I don't want anything. But Laurel deserves to be among those who can help her hone her gifts. She's not meant to be just mine. She's meant to be shared with the world." My chest ached.

"I have some things to consider, Brayden." She paused as though something dawned on her. "You say you drove all the way from West Virginia? Today?"

"Yes ma'am."

"Did you book an Airbnb or a hotel? Surely you are not driving back home."

"I hadn't planned anything past getting up here and talking to you," I said.

She gave a very restricted smile which I felt for

her was as close to smiling from ear to ear as she'd ever get.

"Humor an old lady. Come, let's have some of the best cuisine Boston has to offer while you tell me some more about Laurel and how she'd add to our prestigious program, and you are welcome to my son's old bedroom for the night. Then you can go home after some much needed sleep."

I was half in shock and half hopeful. "I'd be so grateful. Your son wouldn't mind?"

This time she gave a sad smile. "No. He passed away twenty years ago. Your passionate enthusiasm reminds me of him. He was the only other person I knew that had a long-term haptic memory. I've never come across another human being with such a gift, and curse."

"I'm so sorry," I said, and I was. I was beginning to understand that we all had grief inside us, sometimes shared, sometimes kept buried deep where no one could touch it. But grief seemed to bring people together, link them to some kind of higher spiritual power. You couldn't tell by looking at someone what they'd endured, or what they continued to.

"Ms. Markacelli?"

"Yes?"

"I'll gladly accept and only ask one more thing from you," I said, standing up.

"Go on," she nudged.

"Whatever comes out of this, please don't ever let Laurel know that I came here."

Chapter Thirty-One

Summertime Sadness

Brayden

June.
Nothing.
July.
Nothing.
August.
Nothing.

"We have an old friend that lives in the Outer Banks of North Carolina. Corolla, to be specific. He happens to own a few cottages down there. Your mother and I have discussed it and you're almost nineteen. We can't force you to do anything. However, I will not accept you as an apprentice and nor can you work for me until you've spent time away from home," my father said matter-of-factly, hands on hips to emphasize his point.

"What?" I asked in shock. He couldn't be serious.

"You heard me. We don't care if you go to college, stay here—more like come back here, or go find yourself somewhere else. But you have to go figure it out. You staying here day in and day out with no hopes or aspirations to do anything but breath in and out has got to stop."

"You want me to stop breathing?"

"No, smartass," my dad said with an arched eyebrow. "Your mother and I want you to spend some time away from the only thing you've ever known to try and see things a little more clearly. We're hoping you'll gain a fresh perspective."

I knew what he was alluding to. They were tired or sad, or even both of me just existing, not trying to get over the loss of Laurel but somehow get through it. And I didn't know how. I just didn't know how to be. All I could do was allow my body to do what it mechanically would on its own.

Breathe in. Breathe out. Shower. Dress. Eat. The summer was an everyday rinse and repeat routine for the following day, and the next and the next.

"So, what's in Corolla that's not here?" I asked, scrubbing a hand down over my face.

"A cottage. A beach. Hopefully clarity can be found in the salt air," he answered.

I just stared at him.

"This isn't up for negotiation."

"So, you're kicking me out?"

"No. We want you to live, and that can't happen from your bedroom. You're leaving this weekend."

"For how long?"

"As long as it takes," he said.

I never said goodbye. To anyone. I just quietly slipped away that cool Saturday morning.

I drove for nine hours to get to Corolla, North Carolina. In addition to staying at this little beach bungalow cottage, Dad made arrangements for me to work as a crabber on the weekends. As if I'd know anything about crabbing, or deep-sea fishing. I knew about night fishing back home and that was as far as my knowledge extended. I knew of every creek, river, and stream. The sandy landscape with live oaks and rows upon rows of large beach homes was so different from the mountainous terrain with cold mountain air back home.

As I pulled up to the address given to me, I parked and tried the combination lock texted to me. I heard a small click. I opened the door to what appeared to be a one room studio apartment. I walked in and set my bag down. I walked in farther. Not that there was much to explore, but I was a little curious about the place I was supposed to call home indefinitely.

There was a small loveseat with a wicker chair at the foot of a double bed. To the left was a small kitchen sink, equipped with a refrigerator, microwave, coffee pot, and a table for two. To the other side was a small sectioned off closet. Upon further inspection, it turned out to be the smallest bathroom I'd ever seen in my life. There was a stand-up stall shower with a toilet literally so close it looked like you could fall out of the shower and into it.

I stepped back out and surveyed the quaint room one last time. I sat down at the table and noticed an envelope with my name on it. I opened it.

Brayden,

Your dad and I go way back, to like high school days. I've not seen you or your brother since you were little boys. Enjoy the rest of the week. Help yourself to anything in the house. The locals aren't always crazy about tourists down here, so try to blend in. There's a Harris Teeter down the road if you need groceries. Work begins Saturday at 1100 Club Road. It's a big yellow restored 1920s-era Art Nouveau-style mansion, soundside. We dock there and crabbing begins at six sharp. In the morning.

Dan Foster

Okay. So, in a nutshell I was looking for a big, old yellow house. I opened the fridge and there was the six pack of Cheladas. My parents loved them, or at least while we were at the beach they did. I wasn't much of a drinker—really, I wasn't one at all—but I was guessing this was what the locals drank.

I grabbed one, popped another off from the rest of the six pack and took both with me. I walked outside to the front of the cottage. It opened up to sand and the ocean for as far as I could see on either side of me. It was the end of summer, and it looked like there were still several families on vacation.

My parents said it would thin out by September and by November, only locals would remain. I couldn't imagine time, more of this, more of the same, without Laurel. Every day the reality of it sunk in more and more, but the memory of her never faded.

I sat in the sand outside my cottage and stared at the ocean, it's waving laps of foamy sea water crashing ashore and receding back just as fast. I cracked open the Chelada and took a long swig.

Beer, tomato, and clam juice. It was nothing I would've ever voluntarily tried, but that was my life at the moment—a series of things I would've never tried. As I drank it slowly, the calm and quiet made me think of Mrs. McKenzie, but mostly Mr. McKenzie. My thoughts roamed to Laurel's mom. How did they tolerate living after so much loss? I thought about Ms. Markacelli, and the loss of her only son. She told me he died in a car wreck, that she could remember receiving that news as vividly today as though it happened yesterday.

I drank my beer down, ready for another. The strange savory taste was warm in my belly and growing on me. I gave this moment of silence to those who'd grieved. And as the dark crept in all around me, the oddest thing happened.

In the twilight of the ocean breeze, against the speed of the winds, against all odds, a single firefly floated past me.

Chapter Thirty-Two

And Life Goes On

Brayden

December.

It was milder in the Outer Banks than at home, but still chilly. Crabbing turned out to be something I was good at. Baiting up chicken necks and learning how to navigate through the marsh of the sound waters was something I caught onto easily.

And it was soothing.

All these months later, and I still hadn't heard anything from Laurel. At night when I was all alone in my bungalow, I'd fall asleep to the sound of the ocean and Laurel singing. She always was a siren to me.

****

Winter.

Nothing.

Spring.

Nothing.

Summer.

Nothing.

Fall.

Nothing.

Winter.

Nothing.

Spring.

Nothing.

Summer.

Nothing.

Fall.

Nothing.

Winter.

It was time to go home and see my parents. It was

long past due.

Chapter Thirty-Three

Home is Where the Heart Is

Brayden

It felt odd and comforting at the same time to sleep in my bed at home in West Virginia. I'd gotten in late and true to form, my mom had been waiting up for me. She even had a piece of German chocolate cake waiting on me.

"Eat this and get to bed, young man. We will catch up in the morning," she said, leaning on her tiptoes to plant a kiss on my cheek before leaving me.

I woke to the sun breaking through the curtains of my window—a rarity during winter—and yawned. I stared up at the ceiling for a few moments, stretching. Then I threw the covers off to get out of bed. I pulled a shirt down over my head and walked out into the living room where both of my parents were.

"Lord, look how dark you are!"

"Well, it is the beach and when you're there all year round, it's hardly surprising," I said, grinning at my mom.

"I'm jealous."

"You could always come visit me."

"True. And I will, I will. I love the beach. And your father and I need to do that more. It's just been so busy up here and getting the time off to come for more than a weekend here and there has been near impossible. But," Mom started, side-eyeing my dad as though a bit nervous to proceed. "We were wanting to discuss what your plans are."

"What do you mean?" I asked, grabbing a spot on the loveseat facing Mom and Dad.

"Well, we mean, um, do you have any plans of

coming home anytime in the near future or what's going on?"

I'd been gone for two years. I learned how to crab, deep sea fish. I'd learned the ins and outs of the seafood market, and there was a peace that came with it that calmed the storm I always had to keep at bay inside of me. I loved home. Loved my parents. But everything about being home in Buckhannon reminded me of what I'd finally learned how to leave and, painfully, live without.

"I figured I'd spend Christmas here with you guys and then go back," I said, tucking a pillow under my arm.

I could see the slightest trace of disappointment flash across their faces.

"As long as you're happy."

I never answered.

"You are happy, aren't you?" Mom asked. "You know you can always come home. Honey, we just wanted you to explore somewhere else and see if things worked out better for you. We didn't exactly mean for your move to be permanent."

"Nothing is permanent, is it?" I said quietly. I knew they were referring to Laurel, to what happened that God awful night two years ago. It was a small whispering kind of town, and my parents loved me enough to want to save me from the gossip, the cruel whispers about what kind of monster I'd turned into, or a disappointment to my parents the town imagined me to be. And really, I loved them for caring enough. But things settled. Sort of.

The sea sang me a lullaby of sorts as I worked and collected her offerings. There was no remedy for memory. But the sea seemed to help ease the ache my memories created. I could cope. Maybe I'd move home in time. But not right now, I was still working things out.

****

I drove around town. It was odd how much over two years changed things and yet how little at the same time. Against my better judgment, I parked near Main Street and walked down the sidewalk, the same sidewalk where I first heard Laurel.

I walked past Mama Mia's, past where she'd play open mic, and I stopped and stared at the raised concrete flower planter where she would busk. It was cold and empty, but I could still see her, sitting there playing to the crowd. I sucked in a sharp breath and closed my eyes.

Dammit.

I opened them, gave my head a shake, and continued walking until I found myself in front of the Dairy Duchess. It was closed for the season. I thought back to the first time over two years ago when we sat here and discovered who we were.

I finished at the Dairy Duchess and drove up to the high school. I parked outside our football field and sat there forever just staring at the empty field. And I felt empty. There wasn't anything for me here. Everything about this place was something of the past and just made me want desperately to get back to the boat, to the sea, to what I knew now.

I'd make it through the holidays. I had to because regardless, life went on.

****

Aside from living with ghosts and memories, I was happy to see my parents and my brother, Caleb, who was going to graduate from Marshall in the spring. I was going back to the Outer Banks after Christmas. I wouldn't be back until Caleb's graduation. The holidays approached in a whirlwind, my mom and her non-stop baking—which I loved. She really was a wizard in the kitchen. My waistline probably grew by two inches. I hadn't bothered to call anyone I knew. I'd thought about Chase, and kept up with him on social media, but I just didn't have it in me to explain who I'd morphed into. I didn't know if anyone would understand. And I also didn't know that I'd always be like this. All I knew was one day at a time, and I knew that against all odds, the sea soothed me where I couldn't find comfort elsewhere, but being home made me realize I'd become a bit savage.

It was just easier to stay away.

Christmas morning rolled around, and I could hear the house come alive outside my door. I threw the covers off and met the family in the living room.

My mom was so festive with all her lights and trees, just like we were little boys again. Maybe to her we always would be. There were presents under the tree, stockings brimming full of I knew hygiene products and candy—a weird tradition she'd started when we really were little and maintained—and I could smell food I knew she'd had cooking since last night.

"We can snack around while opening presents," Mom said. "What do you boys think?"

"Sounds great to me," Caleb chimed in.

"Perfect. Well, let's see what we have up front here," Mom said, on her knees, reaching under the tree and pulling presents out.

Pretty soon all I could hear was the sound of paper getting ripped and tossed all over the living room mixed with the audible 'wows' once the present inside was finally revealed.

"We hope you boys liked your gifts," Mom said.

I was grateful Caleb at least didn't have his head up his ass like me and thought of our parents. I gave him half the money, but we both—at Caleb's suggestion—bought them a weekend in the Poconos. My parents were the greatest, and I knew in my heart they deserved a better son than the one they got in me. In spite of all my many flaws and failings, they somehow managed to still love me.

"Well, Caleb, where you're getting ready to graduate, we got you things we felt you could use for the remainder of the semester. We hope you aren't too disappointed."

"Are you kidding me? These are great."

"And we have one last thing for you, Brayden," Dad said, standing up.

"From all of us Andersons," Mom added.

Dad walked out of the room, and I could hear the garage door open and close. I couldn't imagine at all what would be out there.

Moments later, Mom said, "Close your eyes."

I felt a bit ridiculous, but my parents' enthusiasm and even Caleb's giddy expression made me comply.

"Hold out your hands."

I relaxed my arms but extended my hands while closing my eyes. I felt a warm, fluffy, living thing in my arms, and felt it rest against me.

"Open them," Dad said.

I looked down into the big, soft, all-knowing eyes of a fluffy German Shepard puppy. I was stunned.

"We know you are alone in that little beach cottage, and if you've made friends, we've never heard you talk about them. We worry about you being lonely. This way, you never have to be again," Mom said with a soft smile.

"We already talked to Dan. He's fine with a pet as long as you take care of him," Dad said, ten steps ahead of me, as though reading my thoughts.

"It's a he, huh?" I said, holding him up closer for me to have a good look at him. I was pretty shocked.

"Yes, it's a little boy. And we picked him out of the litter because of all of them he kept coming back to us and not to play but to sit at our feet. Kind of like he chose us."

I looked down into eyes that were kind, that were intelligent, and emotional, and I remembered the legend that was Zelda, not just the game, but the actual dog that was a legend. Laurel's childhood pet. And as we looked into each other's eyes, part of me wondered in some strange cosmic way if Zelda had worked her way back into the fold.

"What will you name him?" Caleb asked, standing up to come over and scratch him between the ears.

I contemplated in my head, stewing over what to name this little guy. In *The Legend of Zelda*, she sends her nurse maid to find a hero courageous enough to save the kingdom. Link, usually depicted as an ordinary boy, becomes a hero by saving the world through feats of courage.

I'd wondered if Zelda felt, wherever her spirit was, her grieving kingdom, and if she'd sent this boy to be a hero. I could only hope.

"His name is Link."

"Link?" Dad said. "I like it."

"Me too," Mom said.

I felt the smallest shift in weight from my shoulders floating up, up, up. I felt … *lighter*.

"One last thing," Mom said, coming over with an envelope in her hands. "This came for you a few days ago."

I looked down at the envelope in my hands, and I could understand now why they decided to give me the puppy first.

The white, crisp envelope read:

Berklee College of Music

A flood of emotions hit me. Why was I getting anything from there? I stood up with Link tucked under my arm, envelope in hand, and went to my room. My heart was pounding. I sat down on the edge of my bed and let Link roll around behind me.

I stared down at the envelope for what seemed forever before taking enough courage to open it. Laurel was always on my mind. I knew she'd do great things. I hadn't tried contacting her. I never erased my videos of her singing and playing, they were too precious to me for that, but I never attempted to find her, keep any kind of tabs on her. I knew she didn't need or want me in her life, but it was too cruel chasing a ghost. Instead, I always imagined her rising to some kind of glory through Berklee because if I knew anything about Laurel, it was that she aced that second audition. I refused to believe anything else.

With shaky hands, I opened it. It was an invitation. My eyes roamed over the inscription, and I was a bit stunned. The Berklee School of Music would be putting on a special solo performance at the Clay Center in Charleston—a stop they were making on their Eastern tour. There was a roster of nine students, and they were going to nine states. Each student, it appeared, chose which state to complete their solo performance in.

My heart raced looking down at Laurel's name, in a place where a name like hers belonged. The name of her production: *A Nod to Appalachia.* December 29th, 6:00PM, The Clay Center, Charleston, West Virginia.

Behind was a ticket with a small handwritten sticky note attached to it.

She figured it out because she's not an idiot. But you already knew that. The next move is yours. I hope you don't disappoint an old friend. Yours, Ms. Markacelli

SASHA HIBBS

Chapter Thirty-Four

The Truth About Fireflies

Laurel

"You look beautiful!" Dad said, holding me at arm's length, inspecting me. "You look so much like your mama. We are *all* proud of you."

I hadn't even performed yet, but I was my father's girl, and he'd praise me for just existing. And I knew who he meant by all of us—he meant to include my mama. "Maybe you should wait until you actually watch the show. You might cringe. You never know, I might throw a curveball at you."

"I doubt it," he said. "You break a leg, girl of mine. Know your old pa is out there watching you."

I was a little over two years into my study at Berklee School of Music, and mid-way through, a handful of students were selected to write, conduct, play, and perform in their own musical. And really the rules were pretty lax. You had free reign, and I knew being selected was the school's vote of confidence. I was so happy for my peers, but I wanted to bring pride to my home state. I'd worked hard for this night, and my heart was so full to be responsible for the show that was getting ready to be put on.

The governor and first lady of West Virginia would be in attendance, as would the mayor of Charleston—our capital, among other senators and people considered noteworthy. But there was only one I was praying with everything in me was here, watching, waiting, knowing it was never over for me. I just hoped I wasn't too late.

I couldn't believe it. There'd been a trail of heartache that led to this point, but when the ache dulled, and eventually faded away, I could see that there was a whole bunch of love that led up to this point too.

It took me over two years to realize that. I just hoped it wasn't too late. As I left my father and ascended the stage, I knew in my heart I didn't want to be another tragic hero so overcome by grief and loss that I forgot what it was and meant to fully forgive and let go. I was going to give it back tonight—all the longing and loss, the love, the hurt, the beautifully broken fragments of pain that reminded us we were alive, that we could feel, even pain, and be thankful for that.

The grand auditorium fell silent as I took the stage. The only sound was the clicking of my heels against the waxed floor. I looked over my shoulder at the small orchestra assembled here. I had to compose all my pieces months ago and send for select members of the West Virginia Orchestra to learn and play for my special opening night.

I took a deep breath and seated myself center stage in front of a grand piano. My severest critic as well as my biggest cheerleader, Ms. Markacelli, came out gracefully from behind the thick red velvet curtains and situated herself not too far from me. She poised herself in front of the microphone and announced our program.

"Ladies and gentleman, we, The Berklee School of Music, are a proud institution with a long-proven history of greatness. Some of our students have gone on to win Grammys, among many other accolades. We've performed here in your beloved city before." She smiled and played to the crowd. "Go Mountaineers!"

The crowd erupted in applause before dying back down.

"Tonight is the debut of one of your daughters— Ms. Laurel Bennett—in her tribute to a region that, so it would seem, means the world to her. It's our sincerest hope you'll feel the soul of our brilliant student, and your daughter, has breathed into this performance. All musical arrangements are composed by Ms. Bennett. Without further ado, we ask that you give a warm welcome and homecoming to Ms. Laurel Bennett, in addition to your very own West Virginia Orchestra." She waved an arm over us before exiting behind the curtains.

I closed my eyes, allowing my fingers to slide over the cold, hard keys that dared me to strike. And like a match, I lit it up with fire, with passion, with fury. I opened the show with a soft tune, one that beckoned a memory. Behind me, as I struck each key, strategically placed lights flickered, forming a scene of mountains, in the distance, the faintest silhouette of a family—three figures representing me as a little girl holding hands between my parents. I sang our story—one of happiness and the little girl grew, as the mother shrank, but her light grew brighter and brighter until finally she was no longer part of the group but rather the brightest light in the heavens situated over a grown me. My first song ended on a high note, one that was meant to match the soaring heavens my mother was now part of, for I had to go high, high, higher to reach her.

After a few moments of silence, as rehearsed with the orchestra, I sang, opening my mouth and projecting all my pain, my love, my willingness to go back to places I thought were best left in the past once upon a time, and the cellos and violins lit up a trail that outlined the shadow of a dog—not just any dog, but my gorgeous girl who'd gotten me through some of the darkest moments of my life. Lights took on the shape of her, running, running, running as I sang and sang and sang. She ran through the mountains, chased a trail of birds that lit up her path until she, like my mom, grew brighter and brighter until she was among the stars herself.

There were collective gasps of awe from the audience, joyous sounds of approval. I drew courage from their praise, but there was one set of eyes I was hoping was among those in attendance, but more importantly and more than seeing, I hope he heard, all the way to his heart.

I felt I had to go back to the night we met, the night that started it all. It was simplistic, but I pulled out my old ukulele–the instrument gifted to me by my parents, the instrument I played that landed me a scholarship with Berklee, the instrument I played all those many nights ago when I first met Brayden Anderson.

And as I wrapped my fingers around the neck of that tattered instrument, I was thankful for my haptic memory, because I remembered it all. Closing my eyes, I knew as I opened my mouth and allowed the first notes of *I'm So Lonesome I Could Cry* to burst forth, a collage of white lights erupted in the backdrop. A picture painted with lights, the brushstroke of my voice and instrument illuminated the canvas behind me. As I sang what I'd once told the boy I loved so long ago was the anthem of my life, my story—*our story*—came full circle.

The outline of a boy and girl finding each other in the dark shone against the stark contrast of the night. They were searching, searching, searching, until finally … in the dark, their love, longing, pain, all lit up by a path of fireflies, helped them to find each other again.

As the last notes left my heart, navigating upward and to my lips, I opened my eyes, and my spirit was moved at the stunned silence of my audience. I'd accomplished what I set out to do—move people the way I'd been moved, the way I'd loved, lost, and somehow against the odds, found my way to peace. The way I loved my mother, the way I loved Mrs. McKenzie—a beautiful Dulcinea—the way I loved Zelda, the way I loved our beautiful home state filled with rivers and mountains, and the way I loved a boy. But also, my debut was a tribute to how they loved me.

I lowered my ukulele and bowed.

The crowd stood and my ears were met with the thunderous clapping of approval.

Ms. Markacelli quickly appeared on stage and encouraged another round of applause for me and for the orchestra. I had so much to be grateful for. The second chance given to me to belong to a world of music that literally sang to my soul. I'd found the courage to forgive. To forget. To let go of the painful past and grab onto a future that was mine for the taking—I only had to walk forward and claim it.

And I did.

I walked off the stage and went to find my father in the reception area. He snatched me up and hugged me. For a long time, he wouldn't let me go. And in that silence, I felt his pride, his joy, also his grief at the reminder of a woman who'd touched both our lives in such a way it left a permanent mark. I supposed it always would until the day my father was among the stars himself with the love of his life. I didn't need to say anything. I simply wrapped my arms around his waist and clung to him.

"Emily will be sorry she missed this," I said smugly. "I guess she had to be a diva and get stuck in Costa Rica."

"You better believe I recorded the entire show. I'll send it to you, and you can send it to her. I guess if you're going to get stuck somewhere, Costa Rica would be the place to have that happen," Dad said.

"True, true." I missed my cousin and best friend. She was studying zoology abroad and her flight got delayed. We were both knee deep in college and that made it difficult to see each other, but a bond like ours couldn't weaken because time and circumstances took us in different directions. We saw each other when we could and knew things wouldn't be like this forever. When we were little girls, we made a pact to grow up, start a chain lemonade stand business, and live together.

Life took us in different directions, but the thing was, when you loved someone, distance was only a formality. It never really separated you.

"I'll be back. I think I need some fresh air."

"You sure you're okay?"

"Oh gosh, yes," I said, smiling. I stood up on my tiptoes and gave my dad a peck on his cheek. I had the best father in the world. "Just a little cold air. I'll be right back. Promise."

I quickly walked outside to a large balcony-like space with flower planters situated symmetrically apart from each other. I could see my breath, a cloud of translucence that lifted into the night as I looked up at stars, wondering who all was among them and how they'd once touched the lives of those of us down below.

I closed my eyes and sucked in a sharp breath. My heart sank a little believing Brayden had moved on, hadn't made it tonight even though I knew he'd been invited. I was so hurt and lost, blinded by pain I refused to let go of. I could still feel the shock of over two years ago when Ms. Markacelli—who looked incredibly out of place—knocked on my door.

You could've knocked me over with a feather, really a small breath would've been enough to do the trick. But she showed up, tracked me down, and talked to me worse, I'm positive, than any prisoner of war. She scolded me for being lazy, irresponsible, and wasteful. Asked me who did I think I was to overlook such a gift simply because someone said something to me that hurt my feelings.

Just as clear as it was yesterday, she stood in my living room, dressed like a bank CEO, red lipstick, tightly secured bun at the base of her neck, a streak of white hair against otherwise black. She was an intimidating force to be reckoned with.

"You lazy, impudent child!" she began. "Who do you think you are to waste an opportunity hundreds of other kids were passed over due to *you*?"

I stood in my living room, wearing a tattered t-shirt, boxer shorts, looking rough, and I was silenced due to utter shock. It was hard for me to digest what was happening. I couldn't believe the esteemed Ms. Markacelli—a grammy award winning artist, turned Berklee ambassador—was standing in my living room. Berating *me*.

I opened my mouth to speak, to try and formulate some kind of defense. She didn't know me, know my suffering. While I was intimidated by her, I wasn't going to let go of the hurt that made my decision to miss my audition. The insult to my mother's memory was too much for me to bear.

"My mother killed herself. In the living room you are standing in right now. And against my better judgment, against all the whispers and rumors in town that my mom was a drug addict and she overdosed because she was a junky, I swallowed it all down. I went to school. I ignored the talk until the talk finally became whispers, until finally people quit talking about it altogether. And then I met a boy. And I loved him. And he betrayed me," I said, my voice becoming shaky.

"In what way did this boy betray you?" Ms. Markacelli shifted her weight from one high heeled foot to the other.

"He made me love him. Made me believe he'd support my dreams, and when the chance came up to crush me, he did. He hit me where he knew it would hurt. I was trying to tell him about Berklee. Trying—" I choked up. I swallowed hard, tears burning in my eyes. "He mocked the fact that my mother killed herself. My mother wasn't a junkie. She was sick. She was eaten up by cancer. She chose to leave us while we could remember her like she once was instead of what she feared she'd become." I lost all control, openly weeping, hot tears streaming down my face, pelting against my chest.

"So, you honor her instead of *this*." She waved a hand up and down the length of me, her face curled up in disapproval. "It's your responsibility to live. To keep breathing. To contribute to the world the gifts given to you."

"But you don't understand—"

She cut me off so fast, I took a step backward as she came in close, coiled like a snake ready to strike. "Oh, but I do, young lady. Do you know I told my son he was a disappointment to me? That going to trade school to become a welder when he'd been blessed with a long-term haptic memory was a disgrace to me. And my words hurt him. It was just as well my words be razors, slashing at him with each syllable. I could see the hurt of what I'd said staring back at me from the eyes of my only child. And that was the last time I saw him. Those were the last words from my lips to his ears. He died twenty minutes later in a car wreck." She remained composed, and I was speechless. "Do you know what you do with that?"

I shook my head, unable to formulate a counterattack. What could you say to that?

"You live. For them. You breathe because they can't. You honor life. Because it is fleeting, and beautiful, and by God, from the heart of a mother to the one you lost, on the life and love of my only child, my precious, precious son, your mother is looking down now with nothing but sorrow in her heart for your suffering."

I wept and wept.

"Let it go, Laurel. Let it be. I see something of my Ben—Benji is what I called him—in you. Honor your mother as I honor my son. You prove you are worthy of their love by living. Come with me," she said, extending her hand.

I looked down at her extended hand. She had long, slender fingers, red polished nails. She was so elegant. I stood in my living room a wreck staring at a person who gave old Hollywood vibes. And I realized we shared a pain that tied us together. My heart ached. I wondered if my mama sent for her. I took that hand, and I never looked back.

I bowed my head momentarily. I sent up a silent prayer. One for my mama. One for Benji. One for every soul hurt by loving. I closed my eyes, glad to have this moment, this night that against everything almost never happened. I gasped at the feel of something furry rubbing up against my ankles. My eyes flew open.

"Oh my gosh! Where'd you come from?" I bent down, half in shock, and scratched between the ears of the fluffiest German Shepherd puppy I'd ever seen. Those eyes, those big brown saucers melted me. "We've got to find your owner, buddy." My hand tingled where I'd just petted him. Memories burst behind my eyes, memories from years ago, of a farm where there were hives, and bees, and honey, and black fur balls rolling around on the grass. The hand never forgot. Never. "Zelda?" My heart was racing, running, overwhelmed.

I picked up this little soul at my feet and held him close to my heart, scratching between his ears and felt that somehow Zelda wasn't done with me, couldn't rest in peace until she got me through my last challenge.

I turned, holding onto this little puppy with one hand, when suddenly my free hand was grabbed by a rough one that had been subjected to hard labor. Fingers intertwining with mine, taking me back to the night we'd met.

I smiled, closing my eyes, as the happiest memories of my life came back to me in a tidal wave, crashing over me like sunshine, like water against thirsty lips. I saw a boy watching me curiously while I busked on the sidewalk, and then the same boy I helped out by saving him the nervousness of asking me out on a date, so I asked for the both of us. I saw a boy whose gaze turned from curiosity, to shyness, to love staring back at me. I saw a boy in a flannel nervously hoping I'd tolerate night fishing, not realizing I'd tolerate more than that just to be by his side. I saw a boy kissing me at homecoming. I saw a boy watching and listening to me sing as though I was the only person in the world, so swept off his feet was he by my voice. I saw a boy who struggled with how to help someone he loved grieve because he was inexperienced with those kinds of feelings. I saw a boy, who in his desperation to not lose the girl he loved, lash out, causing the very thing to happen he'd been praying wouldn't. I saw a boy in the night, the only light given was by the fireflies flickering around him. And I remembered the truth about fireflies. I knew Brayden's light was one I'd always find, because only I knew it, recognized it.

And then I opened my eyes and saw the boy in my mind had become a man, a man who stood before me with tears shining in his eyes. I could see insecurity in them, fear, and I knew what his gaze meant.

"Brayden—"

"Laurel, can you ever forgive me?"

I let go of his hand and gently lowered the puppy, who, like Zelda, leaned up against my leg, and I brought both my hands up to cup his stubble-covered face. We both had tears in our eyes, a dam of emotions waiting to fall.

"Can you ever forgive *me*?" I whispered against his lips.

"I hurt you in an unforgivable way—"

I cut him off, letting my lips crash against his, swallowing up words that were hard to say, because I loved him. He didn't need to say what I knew he already felt. Our lips moved against each other like long lost lovers.

His arms circled my waist, pulling me into him, closer, closer, closer. I couldn't get close enough. I could feel his warmth, his heartbeat against my own. And I finally felt ... at home.

"Well, I take it you approve of tonight's performance, Mr. Anderson?" I heard Ms. Markacelli say.

We broke apart, still holding onto each other, to look at the woman who I believe the universe sent to us both, to see her arching an eyebrow while giving a coy smile.

"Yes, ma'am," Brayden answered, his voice low, impassioned, warm.

"Well, I would hope so. It took a lot of work to get here," she said, and I knew what she implied. All the pain, all the grief, all the loss to ultimately learn to live and be grateful for life ... it was work. But it was worth every tear, every smile, every heartache. "It's good to see an old friend." She turned on her heels and left us to find our way.

"I've missed you, Brayden." I felt like my heart could burst. I saw nothing but a lifetime awaiting us staring down at me from his gaze.

He leaned his forehead against mine. "His name is Link."

"Link?"

"The puppy. I told him all about you. He found you."

I laughed. "Link's my hero."

And I knew in my heart, that's how Zelda meant for this to play out. She sent a hero to save her grieving kingdom. None of these steps, these moments in life, were irony. I was meant to love each person that had come and gone, and those—like Brayden—who came back into my life. From beyond, the stars brought us back together.

"Laurel?" Brayden whispered against my lips.

"Yes," I answered, so grateful to be in his arms, arms that were like a home I'd never left.

"I've never stopped loving you. I don't care what I have to do. I'll do whatever it takes to make us work. I don't ever want to lose you again."

"You won't. I believe in us." I smiled against his lips, going in to kiss him. "And I suspect the universe believes in us too."

In that moment, two souls merged to sing a song in honor of those who'd worked from beyond to bring us back together. I'd never let my grief define me again. Only love. Only gratitude. I clung onto Brayden and allowed all the love I had to fill me up, to spill out like a waterfall from my heart, knowing he'd feel it too.

"Thank you, Zelda. Thank you, Mama," I said, whispering against the wind that would be carried up into the heavens where those I loved could hear.

The End

Evernight Teen ®

www.evernightteen.com